WHAT

*Grace Livingston Hill*

L I B R A R Y

# WHAT SHE SAID: AND WHAT SHE MEANT

## AND

# PEOPLE WHO HAVEN'T TIME AND CAN'T AFFORD IT

ISABELLA ALDEN

LIVING BOOKS®
Tyndale House Publishers, Inc.
Wheaton, Illinois

*ET*

Visit Tyndale's exciting Web site at www.tyndale.com

*Living Books* is a registered trademark of Tyndale House Publishers, Inc.
Tyndale House Publishers edition 1997

ISBN 0-8423-3194-8

Printed in the United States of America

02   01   00   99   98   97
8    7    6    5    4    3    2    1

# CONTENTS

# WELCOME

*by Grace Livingston Hill*

As long ago as I can remember, there was always a radiant being who was next to my mother and father in my heart and who seemed to me to be a combination of fairy godmother, heroine, and saint. I thought her the most beautiful, wise, and wonderful person in my world, outside of my home. I treasured her smiles, copied her ways, and listened breathlessly to all she had to say, sitting at her feet worshipfully whenever she was near; ready to run any errand for her, no matter how far.

I measured other people by her principles and opinions, and always felt that her word was final. I am afraid I even corrected my beloved parents sometimes when they failed to state some principle or opinion as she had done.

When she came on a visit, the house seemed glorified because of her presence; while she remained, life was one long holiday; when she went away, it seemed as if a blight had fallen.

She was young, gracious, and very good to be with.

This radiant creature was known to me by the name of Auntie Belle, though my mother and my grandmother called her Isabella! Just like that! Even sharply sometimes when they disagreed with her: "*Isabella!*" I wondered that they dared.

Later, I found that others had still other names for her. To the congregation of which her husband was pastor she was known as Mrs. Alden. And there was another world in which she moved and had her being when she went away from us from time to time; or when at certain hours in the day she shut herself within a room that was sacredly known as a Study, and wrote for a long time, while we all tried to keep still; and in this other world of hers she was known as Pansy. It was a world that loved and honored her, a world that gave her homage and wrote her letters by the hundreds each week.

As I grew older and learned to read, I devoured her stories chapter by chapter, even sometimes page by page as they came hot from the typewriter; occasionally stealing in for an instant when she left the study to snatch the latest page and see what had happened next; or to accost her as her morning's work was done with: "Oh, have you finished another chapter?"

Often the whole family would crowd around when the word went around that the last chapter of something was finished and going to be read aloud. And now we listened, breathless, as she read and made her characters live before us.

The letters that poured in at every mail were overwhelming. Asking for her autograph and her photograph; begging for pieces of her best dress to sew into patchwork; begging for advice on how to become a great author; begging for advice on every possible subject. And she answered them all!

Sometimes I look back upon her long and busy life and marvel at what she has accomplished. She was a marvelous housekeeper, knowing every dainty detail of her home to perfection. And a marvelous pastor's wife! The real old-fashioned kind, who made calls with her husband, knew every member intimately, cared for the sick, gathered the young people into her home, and loved them all as if they had been her brothers and sisters. She was beloved, almost adored, by all the members. And she was a tender, vigilant, wonderful mother, such a mother as few are privileged to have, giving without stint of her time, her strength, her love, and her companionship. She was a speaker and teacher, too.

All these things she did and *yet wrote books!* Stories out of real life that struck home and showed us to ourselves as God saw us; and sent us to our knees to talk with him.

And so, in her name I greet you all, and commend this story to you.

*Grace Livingston Hill*

(This is a condensed version of the foreword Mrs. Hill wrote for her aunt's final book, *An Interrupted Night*.)

# WHAT SHE SAID:
## AND
# WHAT SHE MEANT

# 1

## SEED SOWING

HER name was Mrs. Marks and she sat at the time of which I write in her neat little sewing room. Every thing pertaining to Mrs. Marks was neat. She was sewing. This, too, was characteristic of her quiet moments. She could never be accused of eating "the bread of idleness."

She had company—an intimate friend, Mrs. Silas Eastman by name. This lady was a near neighbor and often ran in to have little social chats with her friend.

You would like to form your opinion of their character, by listening to their conversation? This, in a degree, you shall do. I will pass over the weather; suffice it to say that they discussed it in all its present dryness and prospective dampness and disposed of it, turning promptly to that other most fascination topic among married women, viz: hired help.

"Have you a good girl, now, Mrs. Marks?"

That lady paused long enough in her sewing to raise her eyes, and her eyebrows slightly, as she answered:

ISABELLA ALDEN

"What a question, Mrs. Eastman! *Is* there any such thing known in these degenerate days?

"Well, they are scarce, I admit; but now and then you *do* find one who really seems to be a treasure. I just came from Mrs. Streeters, and she tells me her girl is almost perfect."

"How long has she had her?"

The tone is exceedingly significant. Mrs. Eastman feels it.

"Well, only a few weeks to be sure. But, then, if a girl can do well for two or three weeks, why can't she for a longer time?"

"Ah! that is the question; why *can't* she? I have often had occasion to ask that and have never yet been able to answer."

Mrs. Eastman gives a sympathetic little sigh. She is conscious of a desire to have the girl in question hold out well, though she admits a dawning sense of the improbability of it.

"Well, I'm sure I hope this girl will prove one of the rare exceptions. Mrs. Streeter needs good help, if any one does, with her family of little children."

"Who is the girl, Mrs. Eastman?"

"She belongs to a family who have lately moved here. They live down on Water Street, and are quite poor. Andrews, the name is."

"Oh!"

Did you ever hear that sort of "Oh!" pronounced? If not, how is it possible to make you understand how it sounded in Mrs. Eastman's ears? A whole volume of unwritten history was wrapped up in it about the luckless family who were so unfortunate as to bear the name of "Andrews." The history of the grandfather of the Andrews, and the grandmother of the Andrews on the father's side, and a dim suspicion as to the probable

4

history of the great-grandfather of the Andrews, were all comprehended in that awful "Oh!" It induced from Mrs. Eastman the exclamation:

"Why, Mrs. Marks! *you know* the family *don't* you? Aren't they respectable people?"

"Oh, dear me! I hope so, I am sure."

Did you ever hear a person say "I'm sure *I hope* it's all right—" then did you observe a peculiar shake of the head? If so, you know just the sort of intonation and manner that made Mrs. Marks's sentence so effective.

"Dear, dear! But if there is anything really *wrong* you know, poor Mrs. Streeter ought to be told of it. She is so dependent, kept at home with those little children of hers. All she knows about people is what her friends tell her."

"My dear Mrs. Eastman! *haven't* you lived long enough in this world to realize that the most unthankful thing you can do for people is to interfere in any way with their 'help'? I make it a point of honor never to do it."

"But, then, if the girl is really *bad* you know—"

"I don't dare say she *is.* I shouldn't want her in *my* family, to be sure, under the circumstances. But tastes differ. Oh, I have nothing to say against any of them, nor to do with them, for that matter; let well enough alone, I say. If the family are really suffering, the authorities ought to be informed, though why virtuous people should have any occasion to suffer through poverty, in a world so full of work as ours, is more than I can comprehend."

What had Mrs. Marks said against the Andrews family? Nothing, absolutely nothing. Were they dishonest? Who knew? *She* had not breathed such a hint; and you heard her distinctly declare that she *hoped* they were respectable. Yet Mrs. Eastman, as she thoughtfully evolved the matter, wondered what it *could* be, and resolved to lose no time in warning her particular friend, Mrs. Streeter, against her new girl. At the same time it seemed useless to try to pursue the subject further—Mrs. Marks was *so* averse to anything that looked like gossip. She reluctantly dropped it and took up another.

"Did you know that Mrs. Decker's husband is very sick? I hadn't heard of it until I called there yesterday, and I found the bell muffled, and the girl came tip-toeing around the house to ask me to go out at the side gate because the other made a noise. I was very much shocked! The last time I saw him he seemed to be in perfect health."

"I hadn't heard of it," said Mrs. Marks sewing away, calmly, "but I am not in the least surprised. In fact, if I ever expected to hear of anyone's sickness, I may say I expected his."

"Why, pray?"

"Oh, dear me! don't ask me, I never like to descend to particulars about people; it savors too much of gossip, especially when they are people who don't concern me. The man just astonished me, that is all. What doctor do they employ?"

"Dr. Nellis, and I guess he must have spent the night there. Mr. Eastman walked up with him about eleven o'clock, and this morning when he went down to the four o'clock train he said he saw him coming out of there."

"Is it possible that they employ Dr. Nellis! Well, I *am* astonished! I should think they would be the last people who would want Dr. Nellis in their house *under the circumstances.*"

"My dear Mrs. Marks! why not? Isn't he accounted one of the most skillful physicians in town?"

"I dare say he is by those who happen to like him. For that matter there is nothing easier than to build up a name in the medical profession. A little judicious flattery, frequently bestowed, takes the place of wisdom wonderfully well in the minds of some people and atones even for awful mistakes. Dr. Nellis is really adept at flattery I have heard. But I am not of the sort to be influenced in that way. I employ a physician on account of his skill; I don't care whether he is handsome or homely, and he may be as rude as a bear if he will only attend to his business, *always provided that he understands his business in the first place.*"

"Mrs. Marks, you surprise me beyond anything! I always supposed that Dr. Nellis stood at the head of his profession."

"So he may, for all I know to the contrary. He is not *my* physician. I am not a believer in young doctors anyway; they are much more likely to make mistakes than men who have had long experience, and an error in their profession is so often fatal. I'm sure I don't see how Mr. Decker can endure the sight of that man; but the poor man may be so sick that he doesn't know who attends him."

"My dear Mrs. Marks, I wish you felt at liberty to tell me just what *is* the trouble about Dr. Nellis. I am *so* surprised! I should consider it confidential of course."

"*I don't say* there is any trouble with the man. I wouldn't say it for the world. The Deckers have had an experience that would set some people against him for life, but if *they* can trust him again I am sure anybody may. Oh, *I* have nothing against him, nothing at all. I *hope* Mr. Decker will recover. It would be a heavy blow to them if he followed his son so soon."

"Did they lose a son? Why, how long ago? It must have been before they moved here."

"It was when they lived in Portville."

"Portville! Isn't that the place where Dr. Nellis came from?"

"The very place."

"And he was their doctor when they lived there?"

This time Mrs. Marks bowed her head, with her lips drawn in that peculiar pucker which indicates what volumes could be told if she should only happen to let them out of their pucker! But the determined eyes said, she would *never* do it—*never.*

Mrs. Eastman sighed again over her difficulties in acquiring knowledge.

"Well," she said, "I really must go. I act as though I had nothing in the world to do this afternoon but talk with you, and I started out on a soliciting tour. I want to get half through my street if I can."

"Oh," said Mrs. Marks, "that reminds me; I wanted to warn you not to go to the Petersons with your subscription paper."

"Why not, pray? I was depending on them for a good lift; why shouldn't I go there?"

"Because they won't give, and it will only embarrass them to have to decline and add to the talk."

"But why in the world should they decline? You know they are abundantly able to give. I suppose they are really the wealthiest family there is in our church."

"That has nothing to do with it. You will find they won't help a cent toward any scheme which Mr. Beldon favors so strongly."

"Why, Mrs. Marks! their own pastor! Are they offended with him?"

Mrs. Marks sewed away at her flannel for a moment, then raised her eyes with an impressive look and a sigh and said, "I suppose they are."

"But what is it all about? and when did it happen? I thought they were the most intimate friends."

"So they were; but it is something that he has said which has offended them. Of all inconsiderate people with their tongues I do think ministers are the worst. One would think *they* might have the wisdom to be quiet."

"And you don't know what it is that has offended them?"

"Oh, I have my suspicions; but then I am not one, you know, to talk about such things. I must say I don't wonder at the way they feel. Businessmen, you know, have to be very careful of their reputation, else there is serious trouble. I don't suppose he meant to make any serious charge, but, to say the least, it was very thoughtless. There! don't ask me any more about it; I'm sure I hate such things and I don't want to have anything to do with them."

"Did I ever hear the like in all my life!" exclaimed Mrs. Eastman with uplifted hands. "Why, I quite depended on the Petersons to give me a large donation. So you think there is no use in my going there?"

"Oh, none in the world. It might be very unpleasant to you since you are not specially acquainted with them, and, besides, the sooner such things are hushed up the better—that is, if they *can* be hushed up. The Petersons are a very influential family, and they are proud people, especially in a question that concerns their good name. Besides, a church quarrel is really the most difficult thing to handle in the world, and when the minister gets mixed in with it the case is almost hopeless."

"Yes, indeed! that is true," murmured Mrs. Eastman, and she honestly supposed herself to be pretty sure of just what there was to handle.

"Oh, one moment," she said, as she was about to pass down the walk leading to the gate. "Will you be so kind as to give me the address of the young woman who used to sew for you? Phillips, I think, the name is."

"Hattie Phillips; she lives on Third Street, corner of Broad, but don't *employ her,* if that is what you are after."

"Don't? Why, I thought she was quite superior."

"She is a good enough sewer, but there are other things besides sewing, you know, to be desired in a dressmaker, especially if you have to trust her *entirely.* I don't want to injure the woman, of course, though as a friend I advise you not to employ her. No, I won't even say that; you can act your own judgment about it. She may do well for you; I will only say that *I* have had enough of her."

"Dear me! Some of those poor sewing girls are tempted to be dishonest sometimes. I hope she is not one of them."

"Oh! well, we'll hope so, if that will do her any good; though, as you say, there are great temptations in her work. But I am not prepared to say anything about her in that way or any other, except that I shall look elsewhere for my help."

And then Mrs. Eastman did, finally, bid this good woman farewell, and went down the street intent, not so much on the errand which had called her out, as toiling under the weight of new and strange impressions that she had received.

As for the good woman—she went back to her pretty sewing room and sewed the warm flannel sleeve firmly and neatly into the nightgown of Mrs. O'Flannigan's sick child, for she was a woman who often "spread out her hands to the poor."

# 2

## SEED TAKING ROOT

NOW I want you to follow Mrs. Eastman and her "impressions." She stopped with them at Mrs. Willard's, and as in her transit she had passed the Peterson mansion, naturally she was thinking of them. As soon, then, as she had dispatched her errand she began:

"Why, Mrs. Willard, did you know the Petersons were offended with Mr. Beldon?"

"Offended! No, indeed; I supposed they were very intimate friends."

"Well, it seems there is trouble. I didn't know of it until today, and Mrs. Marks was very guarded in what she said; you know she is *dreadfully* afraid of gossip. But she gave me to understand that it was something pretty serious. Mr. Beldon, it seems, has been talking about Mr. Peterson. I should think, from what she hinted, that he had actually accused him of dishonest dealings in his business, or something of that sort. She says they feel dreadfully— won't have anything to do with the Beldons. *She* doesn't blame them, either, for it has made serious times in his business—the *charges* have, you know; and—well the fact is, there is *trouble.*"

"Oh, dear! to have one's minister gossiped about makes the wretchedest kind of work! It is sure to get into the church, and people take sides, and there is no end to the snarl. Really, I think a minister might as well give up, first as last, when it comes to such a state of things. His usefulness is pretty sure to be destroyed. That accounts for the strange way in which the Petersons have been acting. I wondered what took them to the city the very day of our church sociable; and they were not at the parsonage the other evening when the society met there. Now you speak of it, they are not regular at church anymore. I hadn't thought of it before, but don't you know, there have been several Sundays when nobody but Grace and her little brother were in their pew. Dear! dear! What wretched business!"

"The worst of it is," explained Mrs. Eastman, "that Mr. Beldon has talked about it to others a good deal; and his wife, too, I suppose: She is a good deal of a talker, and, besides, she is a very excitable woman, you know. I shouldn't wonder if *she* had said the most—women always *are* indiscreet; but shouldn't you have thought a man in Mr. Beldon's position would have had sense enough to keep such a thing quiet? The Petersons are the most wealthy family in the church, you know, and by far the most influential. I daresay it was about his salary—some discrepancy, or something of that kind; but why in the world didn't the man let it go! What is the use of thinking so much about *money,* anyway!"

"It will make *trouble,* depend upon it," said Mrs. Willard, very impressively.

There is a way of speaking that word which will

indicate that *trouble* of any sort is a very interesting and exciting thing.

I may as well tell you at once that Mrs. Willard, without possessing a bad heart or having the least desire to do actual harm to anyone, was of that class—that are still in existence—who delight in knowing all about other people's affairs and in managing their very interesting *troubles* for them; or, if they may not do that, who take revenge in talking about them and their troubles, everywhere, on all possible occasions. Such being the case, it is a pity that Mrs. Eastman had not taken her *occasions* elsewhere.

Have you observed that while that lady supposed herself to be giving information which had emanated from Mrs. Marks, in reality she did not quote a single sentence of that lady's? She simply quoted *her impression* of what was said, which is nearly always a different thing from quoting what *is said*.

I declare to you that there was not a better meaning woman in all the length and breadth of that town than Mrs. Silas Eastman. She had not the slightest intention of making trouble that bright afternoon, out on her charitable errand. She had not the remotest idea when she reached home, weary with her commendable efforts, that she *had* made trouble. Bearing those thoughts in mind, follow her.

She proved herself not to be a real newsmonger, for she said nothing about the dressmaker, or Mrs. Streeter's hired girl, or Mr. Decker's illness, while at Mrs. Willard's. None of these topics were suggested to her by circumstances. But an hour afterward she found herself at the Misses Walker's door. Miss Mary Walker had just returned from Mr. Decker's.

"He isn't any better," she said, in answer to inquiries, "and I don't believe they have much hope of him."

"What was the cause of his sickness?" asked Mrs. Eastman, suddenly. "Is he an intemperate man?"

"Why, not that I ever heard! What makes you think so?"

Be it observed that Mrs. Eastman had not *said* she thought so; it must have been her *tone* that was answered, not her words.

"Why, Mrs. Marks hinted something of the sort; at least, she said it was no wonder that he had brought himself down. She was not surprised; one who had been going on as he had must surely have expected it would end in some such way."

"I want to know! Why, it must be so, for Mrs. Marks is well acquainted with them. I wonder we have never heard a lisp of it before; but, of course, people keep such things quiet as long as they can. What a shame! He was always such a pleasant man. I'm afraid he is going to die, too.

"I almost know that Dr. Nellis has no hope of him," said Miss Mary. "I met him coming out of there, and he looked very sad and discouraged. He is such a sympathetic man."

"And that reminds me of another thing," exclaimed Mrs. Eastman. "Mrs. Marks says it is the strangest thing that they should employ Dr. Nellis. He made some horrid blunder in the family when the son died; gave him an overdose, I suppose, or the wrong medicine; something of the kind, anyway."

"I want to know! Wasn't that dreadful? Certainly you would think they had had enough of *him!*"

"That is what Mrs. Marks says. She didn't *tell* me it was an overdose, you know; she just spoke of the dreadful accident of which he was the cause; but it must have been something of that kind."

Did Mrs. Marks speak of a dreadful accident? or was it lifted eyebrows and exclamation points that spoke for her?

The subject glanced off from sickness and physicians, and, by a line of transition known to ladies, reached that of dress.

"I don't know who I am to depend on for my spring sewing," Mrs. Eastman said. "I thought of having Hattie Phillips, but Mrs. Marks warned me against her. I am really disappointed, too, for I took a fancy to the girl."

"I thought Mrs. Marks liked her very much."

"She used to, for she told me so herself; but this is something recent. To tell the truth, I think the girl has been stealing from Mrs. Marks. Indeed, from what she said, I am almost sure of it; only I wouldn't like to have it mentioned, you know. Poor thing! She may have been awfully tempted; they say she has a hard struggle to get along."

"Dear! dear! Why, she is a member of our church!"

"Too bad, isn't it? I meant to give her all my work, and I recommended her to several other ladies who were going to have her. I suppose I shall have to take back my recommendation now. I declare I feel bad enough about it to cry."

With this sympathetic sentence she disposed of the dressmaker and her affairs, then settled several other matters of life and death and secured her subscription. Then the nice little lady took a kindly leave and proceeded on her charitable way.

In the course of the next fifteen minutes Miss Mary Walker had occasion to go across the street to a neighbor's house on an errand. It being the season for much dressmaking and sewing of all sorts, the subject came up while she was there, and of course suggested the recent item of news in the line; the immediate result being that the mistress of that house informed her husband at the tea table that he need not look up that Phillips girl for her; she had heard things about her that made her decide to find someone else.

Many more calls did Mrs. Eastman make; her subscription list swelled, so did her stories; not that she had an idea she was telling any; but it was queer how in nearly every place that she called, some of the subjects about which she had that afternoon acquired knowledge came up for discussion. And yet I do not know that it was strange. She was out raising money for the minister; of course it was natural to speak about him, and speaking of him suggested his trouble with the Petersons. Then, of course, everyone was interested in poor Mr. Decker and his family. It was not until the next morning that the thoughtful little woman found time to run over and warn dear Mrs. Streeter about "that Andrews girl."

"But what is the *matter* with her?" persisted Mrs. Streeter, asking the question for the third time. A woman with three children to care for doesn't want to give up a "perfect treasure of a girl" on the "they say" of people in general, especially when "they" refuse to say anything definite. I will not say that Mrs. Streeter would not have been able to throw aside her pastor, her family physician, even her *dressmaker;* but a girl who *cooked* well, and served *tables* well, and was quiet and respectful—that required serious consideration.

"But she really isn't *respectable;* that is—well, I don't know. Mrs. Marks wouldn't speak plainly; you know she is a thoughtful woman and never wants to injure people; but if you could have seen the way she looked when I told her you had an Andrews girl. Dear Mrs. Streeter, do get rid of her; I'm sure I shall not sleep nights for thinking of her with your children."

"If I only knew what there was against her," Mrs. Streeter said thoughtfully. The *mother* in her stirred. "Suppose I ask Mrs. Marks just what she *does* know about her?"

"Oh, don't; she will think I ran to you telling tales. She wanted me not to interfere; but I thought, since we were such old friends, it was nothing more than right."

Does it need telling, the fact that Mrs. Streeter dismissed her without any special recommendation, either? At least when the poor girl, a stranger in the town, referred those who questioned her to Mrs. Streeter as the woman with whom she had lived for three pleasant weeks, that woman, when inquired of, said she liked the girl very much indeed; never had anyone who had worked better and been so neat and so respectful; but, the fact was, she had heard some unfortunate things about her—nothing very definite, to be sure, but enough to make her feel certain that she had better get rid of her as soon as possible. And Mrs. Streeter, by reason of the *little* that she had to tell, unconsciously pieced it out with wisely ominous looks and expressive silences. *And it worked mischief for the girl.*

I am not disposed to speak slightingly of my sex; I am not disposed to admit that they are, as a class, hopelessly given over to gossip. I have all due respect to the remembrance that I am a woman. Yet, perhaps, one who has studied human nature very much is obliged to own that women interest themselves in the affairs of other women, and of other women's children—yes, and of other women's *husbands*—as men do not.

It is not necessarily a humiliating confession, either; it has its rise in an intense sympathy with humanity— the neighborly, gracious friendliness which men have not the time nor the thought to bestow. It sinks into the mire of common gossip among those women who, letting go the motive and ignoring other studies, cultivate that trait for the sake of the curiosity which it feeds.

Half the difficulty with our women—especially our *young* women—is that they do not read; they are not posted as to what is going on today, either politically, morally, or socially. I do not speak of the army of honorable exceptions who are as interested in all the great questions of life and are as earnest and sacrificing and as patient as any name honored among philanthropists. I do not even speak of that army of exceptions who, by reason of the necessity that is upon them, make life a daily round of incessant drudgery in order that they and their families may be fed and clothed.

It is rather of that class—not small—who, having leisure in a degree, and talents in a degree, and opportunities lying around them, yet belittle their lives and fritter away their brains over the dress question, or the amusement question, or the social, idle gossip which has for its motive, from beginning to end, merely the satisfaction of inordinate curiosity.

Yet, I have taken as the exponents of this way of living not even the extreme class, but a grade above them. The Mrs. Marks and the Mrs. Eastmans of the world, who are virtuous women, keepers at home, industrious, frugal, charitable, refined, intelligent—

those of Mrs. Mark's stamp—have fallen into the habit, insensibly, oftentimes, of speaking or exclaiming ill of everyone who chances to be brought up for conversation.

Such do not so much err in telling *more* than they know as they *appear* to keep back volumes which they *could* tell if they deemed it prudent, and generalize over what *may* be until they succeed in making you believe that it *is*.

What are the motives of such woman? What was Mrs. Marks's motive? She was not aware that she had any. It began in a disposition to look on the dark side of other people's doing, to see a great deal where little was meant. In short, it began with that disposition, which in its earlier, less offensive stages, we pronounce farsightedness. It developed through the desire, natural to the human heart, to be the bearer of news—of good news, if possible—in the beginning of the attack; but, if persistently yielded to, then of news, whether good or bad. Gradually there proves to be more excitement gotten out of the bad than the good; and gradually (shall I say it?) we must have news anyway, even if we manufacture some.

I do not mean that Mrs. Marks had consciously descended to that plane; she even had, in a vague way, a fear of saying too much, and so left her sentences half complete, and retired into the exclamatory realm, or the realm of unutterable looks which meant volumes. This habit was growing on Mrs. Marks.

As to Mrs. Eastman, she has her counterpart in every town and city; she meant nobody any harm; she listened to talk and jumped at conclusions. She had a vivid imagination; she interpreted shoulder shrugs, and lifted eyebrows, and "ohs" and "indeeds" in a royal way. They so promptly took shape and form to her, that it seemed simply impossible that they should mean anything else than they meant to her, and a week afterward she was sure that the very language had been used. Such people are numerous, are the best natured, most sympathetic people in the world, and *make worlds of trouble.*

# 3

## THE SOIL WELL WATERED

I WANT you to attend the sewing society connected with the Second Church of this nameless town. All the people whom we have met were connected with that church. Not all of them were present. Mrs. Marks did not attend; she had sewing enough to do at home; she "looked well to the ways of her own household." And, besides, she thought sewing societies were centers of gossip, and she despised gossip.

The ladies were gathered in little cliques and grades according to their tastes. There were those who were deeply interested in the lecture given on the previous evening, and whose criticisms would certainly have done credit to any of the other sex. There were those who were deep in the discussion of domestic matters—the best jars for fruit canning; what proportion of sugar should be used; whether, after all, canned fruit was so much better than the old-fashioned "pound for pound;" whether oysters were better cooked with milk or without; whether jellies should be boiled long or short and strained in a flannel or a linen bag; whether bread should be kneaded an hour by the clock, or scarcely kneaded at all.

These and a hundred other kindred mysteries pertaining to the department which requires brains and skill and patience and long continuance in well-doing to return fair results, and even then you cannot hope to succeed unless you have that indescribable, untransmittable quality of brain or nerve which housekeepers characterize by the word *knack*.

There were those who discussed with relish and talent the scientific news of the day, who had real and strongly pronounced opinions of the Darwinian theory, and the Huxleyan theory, and all the rest of the monkey theories. Nay, there were those who compared notes with relish and with skill over that modern giant among the intellects, Joseph Cook.

There were those who kindly, sympathizingly, delicately, entirely within the realm of Christian courtesy, discussed the saying and doing of their friends and neighbors. But there were undeniably those who bent their heads and sank their voices into whispers and reveled in the slime of the talk which almost invariably begins with a sepulchral "Oh! *have* you heard what horrid things 'they say' about—" well, about *anyone* who may have chanced before the public in a sufficiently interesting form for that style of vultures to feed upon. As I desire you to join yourself to this latter class, please listen:

"Isn't that the greatest story about the Beldons and the Petersons? I declare I think Mr. Beldon has acted abominably. *I* don't want to hear him preach anymore. I should think the Petersons would want to move away."

"Well, now, what *is* the truth of that? I have heard so many stories I really don't know what to believe."

"Dear me! I hardly know; I guess nobody understands it very well; only they know that Mr. Beldon accused Mr. Peterson of making false entries in the church account and pretending he had been paid his salary when he hadn't. And they had an awful quarrel about it. Some say that if it hadn't been for Mrs. Peterson they would have come to blows. Anyway, Mr. Beldon used *horrid* language. They say he was so angry that his face was as white as a corpse!"

"Oh, my! What a way for a minister to act."

"I know it. Just think! And then they say he told Mr. Peterson that *he* wasn't the only one who had discovered his villainy; that everybody knew he had forged a name once and was only let off by paying an immense sum of money."

"Why, the *idea!* I never heard that before. Do you suppose it is true?"

"Oh, I dare say. Rich men have often been caught in just such things. But I don't see what was the use in Mr. Beldon raking the whole matter up and making such a horrid fuss. It will just drive away the Petersons from the church, of course, and I think it is a real shame; they always give such lovely lawn parties and festivals for the church, and they entertain company so delightfully, anyway. It will just be horrid if they move away."

"I hope they will send of Mr. Beldon and get a new minister. One or the other of them will have to go; the same town won't hold both those families long. Why, they say Mrs. Beldon talked worse, if anything, than her husband. I heard that Grace Peterson was so frightened at the way that she went on that she almost had fits."

"Why! the *idea!* Did you *ever hear of such a thing!* I should think she was a lovely minister's wife!"

"I don't believe a dozen words of the whole story." Thus spoke Miss Nettie Golden, the youngest and quietest of the group. "People gossip so horribly nowadays that you can't believe anything."

"Oh, but this is true! Why, I *know* it to be a fact; I had it on authority that is not to be disputed. It is a horrid enough way for any decent people to act; but for a minister and his wife! I think it is a perfect disgrace to our church."

This is only a taste of the remarkable dish of talk that was served up among those young ladies, members of Mr. Beldon's congregation—some of them members of his Bible class. The stories grew with each repetition of them, as one and another not so well posted as the leaders asked for particulars. Mr. Beldon was "horridly angry," and "used dreadful language," "perfectly awful," and "so did Mr. Peterson; but then he was not a minister; it was not so strange in him, and Mr. Beldon charged him with all sorts of wickedness and said that he had been cheated and slandered and insulted and that he would have revenge if it sent Mr. Peterson to state prison."

*And what would you give for the pastor's influence among those young ladies, after an hour of talk like that?*

Every one of them were *young* ladies. They had not the cares and dignities of housekeeping and wifehood and motherhood to occupy them. Their education had run to daubs of paint on canvas—third-rate daub, you understand—and everlasting third-rate thrumming on pianos, with a smattering of French thrown in to make up the hash. They were not developed in any one direction, consequently they had given themselves over to dress and parties and beaux. In the intervals of rest from these absorptions what is their occupation but knitting and gossip? They talk on:

"I do feel so sorry for the Deckers. They say his illness commenced with an attack of delirium tremens. Isn't that perfectly awful! And he was always thought to be such a nice man!"

"And I heard that Dr. Nellis made the horridest mistakes in his treatment. It was almost like murder; and you know he did murder the son."

"Why, Nellie Eastman!"

"Well, it is just about the same thing. He gave him a dose of the wrong medicine that poisoned him, and he died in two hours afterward—never spoke again. Mrs. Marks told my mother all about it. *Oh,* that horrid man! *I* wouldn't have him to doctor a cat."

"Very few people do have him. They say he has lost practice fearfully. Papa says he shouldn't wonder if he would have to leave town."

"Good for him; I think he ought to go. Oh, girls, I heard such a horrid story yesterday about that Andrews girl. They say she poisoned herself because she couldn't get any work and people thought she wasn't respectable. She almost died. They had two doctors there all night."

"Oh, horrors! But she isn't respectable, is she?"

"Well, no, I suppose not; everyone seems to think she isn't, though nobody understands just why. I guess she has behaved well enough since they lived here. I suppose it was before they moved here. Such things follow one, you know. Milly, do you thin this shade is prettier than the purple for the cross?"

"Rather; I think it more appropriate for a cross. Is the girl going to die?"

"Oh, dear! I don't know. I hope not; such things make one feel so awfully gloomy. I can't get over them for days. Hand me the pink silk, Kate. Girls, there's Dr. Nellis going by. How solemn he looks. I should think he would want to wait until after dark before he walked out."

There was a sudden hushing of tongues and a moving to make room for a newcomer. Mrs. Frank Truman, rightly named if ever a woman was: frank, sunny, keen, sharp as a needle when occasion required, true as steel always and everywhere. She was power in the church and in the town and wherever her influence touched. She sat down on a low hassock right in the center of the group of tongues.

"May I come, girls? I overheard some of your talk, and I want to ask you about it. I have been away, you know, and I don't understand about some of these things which seem to have developed since my absence. What makes you think that Dr. Nellis made a fatal mistake once in giving medicine?"

The girls gave a little startled glances at each other and were silent. They were not accustomed to being asked straightforward questions. At last one ventured.

"Why, everyone says so, Mrs. Truman."

"What 'everyone' says, my dear Milly, is too large to be investigated. What I want is a responsible name."

"Well, Nellie Eastman says her mother was told so."

"She was," Nellie said. "Mrs. Marks told her all about it; she used to know them before they moved here."

"Mrs. Marks! Very well; thank you, Nellie. That name should be responsible, certainly. Now let me ask you why you think that Mr. Decker's illness commences with delirium tremens?"

"Why, it is the general talk, Mrs. Truman, all over town."

"So I perceive. The question is, how came it to be? Who started it? Who knows it to be so?"

These questions the girls could not answer. None

of them knew who said it first, though somebody must have started it, of course. But question and cross-question as she would, she could get no positive knowledge from any one of the group, nor were they able to direct her to any positive source for knowledge. She dropped those two stories, and took up the one which concerned their pastor. Here it was even worse. "They" said it, and everybody believed it. This was the utmost that these girls knew. Even the one who had so earnestly affirmed that she knew it on authority that was not to be disputed remained silent until directly interrogated, and then she admitted that she did not mean she absolutely *knew* it, but only that the one who told her seemed to be so sure of its truth and knew so much about it that she felt as though it must be true.

Here one of the group came to her rescue.

"Why, Mrs. Truman, *everybody* believes that. Look how the Petersons act. They stay in the city half the time, and they are not regular at church anymore than they are at home, and they don't come to society at all."

"My dear," said Mrs. Truman, laying a cool, firm hand on the eager girl's arm, "is all that *proof* of the solemn charges which you have been making against our pastor, or is it unjust and unjustifiable surmise?" And then, to the silenced group, she added:

"I am convinced that there has been a chain of lies formed somewhere. Who started them or what the object would have been, I am at a loss to know, but I mean to discover. I am going to depart from my usual custom and descend to be a bearer of news. I have known Dr. Nellis ever since he was a little boy. He has been intimate with the Deckers for fifteen years. He was indeed the family physician at the time they lost their little son, but he was not even in the same city during the sudden and violent illness. He was telegraphed for, but arrived too late. However, there was not a sort of blame attached to the physician in attendance. He did everything that it was possible for human skill to accomplish. So you see, there is not even *that* foundation for the story. And now think what injustice has been done a skillful physician, a comparatively young one, too, who has his reputation, in part, to make!

"To further prove to you how utterly absurd the story of his mistakes in Mr. Decker's treatment is and the falseness of the report that Mrs. Decker will not speak to him now, I have only to tell you that he is very soon to be married to her youngest sister, and she is to receive them into her family. As to the reports concerning Mr. Decker's habits and the cause of his illness, I haven't words to express my indignation. That decent people, who have lived in the same town with a good man for twenty years, watching his blameless life and his Christian liberality, should in such a cold-blooded way help to circulate a vile slander, originating none of them know how or where, is a disgraceful comment on human nature. But you will remember that I am an intimate friend of Mrs. Decker. I promise you I am not going to let her husband's name go down to the grave thus insulted.

"As regards our pastor and his wife, I have nothing to say *today*, but you will hear more about that matter before long. If people will talk they must take the consequences. I heard what some of you were saying and thought perhaps you could help me in my efforts to reach the truth. But I see you cannot. You are swimming through that dreadful pool of slime 'they say.' Of all irresponsible persons, that every-lastingly quoted 'they' is the most so. Never trust your characters to her, girls, or soil your tongues by repeating her gossip. I want you all to reflect a moment as to what possible proofs you could give concerning the statements that you have been making to each other. Suppose you were in a court of justice, testifying under oath, what *could* you say? It is unworthy of you, girls."

Saying which, she moved away, and the silence that she had made fall on them was broken at last by Nellie Eastman, who said:

"Isn't she horrid?"

And then they fell to wondering who could have told such *perfectly horrid* stories about Dr. Nellis; and declared, each one of them, that *they* had never more than half believed it. And as for Mr. Decker, everybody knew that he was a good man. For their part, they thought it was *perfectly awful* to talk so about people. And they actually did not realize, poor surface dolls that they were, that their silly tongues had eagerly helped in the circulation of the "perfectly horrid stories."

# 4

FRUITAGE

IN order that you may understand the source of Mrs. Frank Truman's courage and the extent of her indignation, I shall have to ask you to go back to a morning preceding the society and make three calls with her. They were to the houses of trouble; yet trouble in more different forms could hardly be found. First she sought, on the decent street where she had left her, for a favorite sewing girl of hers, Hattie Phillips. She did not find her there; but patience and perseverance, and the mounting of two flights of rickety stairs, brought her at last to the dingy back room where Hattie sat and sewed on that which is know as "slop work." But she hummed, and the words that she tenderly lingered over were these:

> When the woes of life o'ertake me,
> Hopes deceive and fears annoy,
> Never shall the cross forsake me;
> Lo! it glows with peace and joy.
> Bane and blessing, pain and pleasure,
> By the cross are sanctified;

*Peace is there, that knows no measure,*
*Joys that through all time abide.*

What were attics, or rickety stairs, or slop work to one who could sing that song with the spirit and with the understanding!

"Why, Hattie!" Mrs. Truman said, "I had a great time finding you. What are you doing here? And making shop shirts, I declare, for a dime apiece, is it? What is the meaning of all this?"

Hattie's kind, gray eyes looked from their clear depths into her questioner's face, as she said:

"It means an honest living, Mrs. Truman; I am going to earn my bread to the best of my strength. There's many a poor soul who can't get this to do."

"But I want to understand what it is all about."

"Why, you see," and there was actually a gleam of mischief in the gray eyes, "the shopmen know that I can't very well steal a sleeve out of a shirt, so they trust me; and by that means I earn my bread and milk; for I will have milk, you know, even if I have to get it in a rusty pail and bring it up these creaking stairs."

"Hattie!" said Mrs. Truman, almost in indignation, "how can you be so bright and funny over such an abominable state of things as this?"

"Dear Mrs. Truman, why not as well laugh as cry? though I won't deny that I have had my turn at crying; but I knew it would all come out right. 'Not a sparrow falls,' you know, without our Father, and I knew that my good name was of more value to him than many sparrows. Besides, it really has its funny side; think of my stealing breadths of silk from Mrs. Marks and the others! What would I do with them?—why don't they think of that?" and this strange girl actually laughed. "Not but that I am glad enough that you have come home," she said, when her laugh was over. "And I haven't been as mild over it as I might, some of the time; but it will end right, somehow. I do wonder really what it is intended to do for me; *something,* of course. What can it be? I suppose I have said a hundred times in the last two weeks: 'All things work together for good.' And I have wished that I could just have a minute's peep behind the scenes and see this queer story in all its snarls and twists working together for my good! Wonderful that it is so, isn't it?" Then she broke down again and her gray eyes filled full of tears, and she dropped her head suddenly on the shoulder of the woman who had been a lifelong friend to her and murmured: "I felt sure you would come this morning. I begged of him to send you."

From there Mrs. Truman went to her old friend, Mrs. Decker. What a house that was to visit! *Crepe* streaming from the doorknob, hush in the hall, servants tip-toeing in that strange, quiet way in which they instinctively move in the presence of death, as if they could disturb the *dead!* The front parlor closed and darkened, mirrors shrouded, easy chairs wheeled back; order and solemnity and gloom pervading the very atmosphere. And *one silent* occupant; forever folded hands, forever pulseless breast. Reverently Mrs. Truman drew back the white covering and looked on that familiar face on which death had set its solemn seal. There was a step behind her, and the wife who had walked with him for twenty years came and stood beside him, looking with dry eyes and a drawn, almost fierce face at her blessed dead.

"The worst is," she said, speaking in a dry, hard tone—"the very worst is, that they *lie* about him! They dare to say that he died because he was, in secret, a drunkard—my husband! Mrs. Truman, think of that!"

Mrs. Truman drew back her head, and with flashing, indignant eyes asked:

"Who says it?"

"Everyone. I hear the servants' chatter, though they do not mean I shall. Isn't it too hard to bear, Mrs. Truman?"

"Oh, no," and Mrs. Truman's voice was sweet and tender now. "Oh, no, dear Mrs. Decker, it isn't. If it were *true,* it would seem almost too hard to bear; but when you and he know what he was, and what he is today, and the dear Lord knows and has called him to come up higher—why, it can be borne, and in a sense, it is as nothing. But I promise you this, Mrs. Decker; it will be taken back. It had its starting point in some silly misstatement or misunderstanding of some sort, and that starting point shall be found. Meantime, it hasn't hurt *him,* you know, and all his friends know it to be as false as it is foolish."

Passing out of that house she almost ran against Dr. Nellis. He held out his hand to his old friend with a warm smile.

"We are passing through deep waters, Alice," he said. She held his hand in a warm grasp of hearty sympathy.

"He was like your brother," she said tenderly. "I know how it hurts.—Oh, yes, I have heard the absurd story.—I hope you don't allow *that* to disturb you? I shall contradict it, of course, and yet it is hardly worthwhile; it is too silly to be believed. But I'm going to find out where all these strange ideas started from, just as a matter of personal curiosity, if for no other motive."

She had another call to make; it was at the home of

"that Andrews girl." What a wan, worn, well-nigh lifeless face it was! And what a rush of strong fresh air, and life, and hope came into the desolate little room with the entrance of Mrs. Frank Truman!

"I'm ashamed of you," she said heartily. "When you get well again and come to live with me, I shall scold you hard, you may be sure of that."

Then the girl cried. She had been proof against reproaches, proof even against her mother's frightened tenderness during the horrors of the night.

"I was so very, very wretched!" she murmured. "You don't know, you can't think what it is to be so deserted and not know what about; I didn't know what to do."

"Nonsense! There were a dozen things to do. Why didn't you ask Mrs. Streeter in plain English what was the matter, and persist until you reached a starting point, then you would have discovered that it started in nothing. Why didn't you write to me and tell me you had been discharged? Why didn't you write to your old pastor and ask for a certificate of good character? Don't you see how many things there were to do, instead of which you did the only dreadful thing of your life—*tried to take it into your own hands and go to meet God before he called you.*"

The girl hid her face in her hands and cried harder. The sore which she had nursed all winter was being probed, roughly, it would seem, but Mrs. Truman had the doctor's word for it that an outburst of natural feeling would be the best thing for her.

"I lost my senses for a little while," she said timidly. "Indeed, Mrs. Truman, I would never have done *that,* if I had known what I was about; but I was wild."

"I dare say; in fact I know it, my child. I don't mean to scold you now. I shall save that, as I told you, until you get well, then you are to come and live with me; and I wish you would hurry, for I am waiting for you. I must go now; and, Jennie, I want you to think of this: God has been very good to you in sparing your life and not letting you in your wildness rush into his presence uncalled. To show your gratitude you must do everything that you can to get well and strong and prove to the world by your future living that you are one of his own. And remember, after this, that one who belongs to the Lord Jesus Christ and is actually looking forward to a home with him for all eternity has no right to be utterly cast down or made desperate by *anything*."

Then this woman bent and left on the pallid forehead a kiss as light and tender as the dropping of a rose leaf. And strength came with it into the very life-blood of the lonely disheartened girl.

"Inasmuch as ye did it unto one of the *least* of these," said the Lord, "ye did it unto me."

It was several days later when Mrs. Truman, who meantime had been very busy running to and fro, made her way into the sunny south parlor of the parsonage. A welcome visitor was she at that home. Do you need to be told that such a woman had strong, granite friendship for her pastor and his family?

Into the midst of the eager questionings and answerings that indicated vivid interest in whatever pertained to the lives of each, Mrs. Truman suddenly broke in with the question:

"By the way, what is the trouble with the Petersons?"

The clear light on her pastor's face gloomed, and instant sadness and anxiety overspread it.

"If you can answer that question for us," he said, quickly, "you will confer another lasting favor. We have no more idea than the wind *what* is the trouble; that there *is trouble* we see plainly enough. They have ceased coming to the parsonage; they declined our invitation only last week, and they have ceased inviting us to their home, which was always open to us, you know. If I should attempt to tell you what infinite pain this has caused us I could hardly succeed. Sometime I even felt that it would necessitate our breaking loose from all these ties here and going out to a new home. The friendship between us has been so strong and the break is so mysterious that it cuts deeply."

Mr. Beldon spoke with strong feeling, with a visible tremble of lip and a perceptible quiver of voice. As for his wife, she silently wiped away large tears as they slowly dropped on her hand. Mrs. Truman looked from one to the other with a puzzled air, in which vexation and amusement blended curiously.

"Do you mean to tell me," she asked at last, "that you have let this thing fester and rankle until it is a raw sore, without ever going to the fountainhead and asking squarely what *is* the matter?"

The pastor wriggled in his chair and looked embarrassed.

"Well, yes," he said, "that is about what we have done, perhaps. The fact is, I didn't see my way clear to speaking with Mr. Peterson. You see there has been nothing pronounced—nothing open, I mean. The trouble is perceptible only to us. Mr. Peterson is too much a gentleman—and in fact the entire family is too well bred to treat us other than courteously in the presence of others. And it—well, the truth is, it seemed to me rather a delicate business to go to a man and say, 'Look here, why don't you invite us to your elegant home to enjoy your elegant hospitalities as heretofore? A man has a right to choose his guests, and to weary of them for that matter, I suppose."

"What an idiotic world it is!" burst forth Mrs. Truman. "And you actually believe that this matter is between yourselves! Pray, where do you suppose I heard of it? My dear pastor, it is all over town; and if you don't know Mr. Peterson's grievance, it is high time you did. I shall not spare your feelings in enlightening you. I have to inform you that you have had 'a horrid quarrel' with Mr. Peterson, or 'a perfectly dreadful time,' or 'a regular row,' according to the degree of refinement possessed by the person who talks about it; that you were 'fearfully angry,' and called dreadful names, and all that sort of thing; that you accused Mr. Peterson of cheating you out of salary due you and hinted broadly that he had, in his earlier days, been a forger, and, oh, dear me! I don't know what *horrid* things you *didn't* say! There was 'a perfectly awful time!'"

"And you helped, Mrs. Beldon; you come in for your full share, I can tell you. And Grace Peterson 'fainted, she was so frightened.' Some have it that way, and some that she tore your hair and bit your arm, or something of that sort. It all seems to depend on the dramatic power of the person who is your informant for the time being. But I'm sure, Mr. Beldon, after all this, you cannot blame the Petersons for not inviting you to dinner."

I will not attempt to describe to you the faces of Mr. and Mrs. Beldon during this rapid recital, that was purposely given a seriocomic air by the reciter. In truth, she could hardly refrain from laughing, partly owing to excitement and partly to the ludicrous changes of expression on her pastor's face from bewilderment to dismay and indignation, and then back to fogginess.

"Did you never hear the story that was told the little boy, with a promise that it should not end until he was weary of it?" she asked at last, after she had almost vainly tried to explain to them the growth of the marvelous gossip. "It was about a snowball which a boy made once upon a time, and it runs in this way: Then he rolled it over, and it grew bigger, and he rolled it over, and it grew bigger, and so on, and on, until tradition says the boy was actually tired, though that I don't believe. But that's the way with this story. It has been rolled over, and over, and over, and grown bigger with every roll, until the original has disappeared in space and left this monster. However, I have the satisfaction of being able to tell you just who rolled it next, and next, and next, and going backward it unwinds beautifully."

"But the original!" said the minister impatiently. "Who could have started such a story, and what could have possibly been the motive? Why, I haven't an enemy in the world, so far as I know."

"Ah, yes, you have; and it is my duty to inform you that it is lurking in your home at this minute. Your own luckless tongue, Mr. Beldon, gave the first start to this magnificent ball!"

# 5

## THE CONCLUSION OF THE
## WHOLE MATTER

"MRS. Truman, do you mean you suppose—"

"Mr. Beldon, I mean I *know* that your own words are the starting point. 'Out of your own mouth will I condemn you.' Listen. Didn't you, once upon a time, in Mrs. Marks's parlor, say that Mr. Peterson had a remarkable way of managing matters as related to the salary—a way peculiar to himself, so far as you knew?"

"Why, I dare say I may have used just that language; but, my dear madam, Mrs. Marks and everyone in our congregation knows just what that meant. They have heard a dozen times over that when there has been an empty treasury on quarter-day, Mr. Peterson writes out his check and sends it to me, precisely as though the treasury was full. And, that when there has been a deficit of the year's account, his hand has invariably gone into his pocket and made it straight. These things are no secrets."

"I can't help it; I am ready to prove to you in court, if you really want me to, that this is the original ball, and that the monster unravels down to it; that is, you have a piece of it. But didn't you further say, on the same unfortunate evening, that Mr. Peterson possessed a dangerous talent in his ability to imitate even the most peculiar handwriting, and that you had known men as high in position and apparently as strong in character as he, ruined in the moment of temptation by such a talent?"

"I—yes, I certainly did make that remark; I remember it. But, then, what of *that*? How was it possible to make anything of such a common statement?"

"Why, it rolled, I tell you, and rolled, and grew bigger and bigger, and was in a fair way never to end—what with your meekness and the world's impishness. But you have the *facts* as sure as I am Mrs. Alice Truman, and I can give you the unwindings."

At this point Mrs. Beldon made her first remark.

"What could have made Mrs. Marks so cruel! We have never offended or injured her, surely."

Mrs. Truman turned to her quickly.

"My dear Mrs. Beldon, there never was a more amazed woman than this same Mrs. Marks. She hadn't an idea that she started this ball. She repeated a word or two that your husband said, according to her abominable fashion, then she retired behind mystery and hints. 'Mr. Beldon had known some very strange things to occur in his day. Mr. Peterson was only human. There were temptations in his line of business that were peculiar. He had full control of the salary, and it was managed in an unusual manner, Mr. Beldon said so himself.' Can't you hear the woman? The Petersons got hold of the ball, after it had rolled just a little further. It appeared to them in the form of a grave hint of possible errors in management and a fear of temptations too strong to be resisted. Naturally they didn't like it; but for fear of making trouble in the church, 'injuring the cause' and all that sort of stuff, they simply kept still and grew hurt and dignified over it instead of coming directly to you as they ought. I hope I shall never be so overburdened with a fear of doing injury to the cause that I shall take leave of my common sense. But, then—Mr. Beldon, where are you going? I'm not half through."

"I'm going to Mr. Peterson's office," said Mr. Beldon, reaching for his hat and making long strides across the hall.

"Just where you ought to have gone two months ago," called out Mrs. Truman after him, as the gate clicked in the lock.

"In fact," said that same brisk lady, not long afterward, as she laughingly closed the account of some household matters to a special friend of hers, who, with her husband was taking tea with the Trumans, "I have my family reconstructed on a basis that is very pleasant. What with Hattie Phillips upstairs, ready to sew on buttons and strings, and darn and hem and tuck, and pull all sorts of wrong things right; and Jennie Andrews in the kitchen to look after matters generally in a way that she understands, I am a woman of comparative leisure and unbounded satisfaction."

"Was that Jennie Andrews who waited on table?"

"Yes. Isn't she neat and skillful and pretty? She is a grand girl. I feel sometimes as though I ought to send poor Mrs. Streeter a note of thanks for discharging her."

"Was there any foundation for that wretched story which they had about her?"

"Why, yes, there was *foundation,* if you can make the story stand on it. The poor child was engaged to marry a man who proved worthless, deserting her on the very night when the marriage was to have taken place; and a great deal of cross-questioning drew from Mrs.

Marks, with whom the story started, the fact that *she* feared he would be hanging around and give Mrs. Streeter trouble. That's the foundation! Don't you wonder the building reached such large proportions? I tell you, I feel enraged when I think of the way that woman talks and looks and exclaims! Only think of the commotion she has raised in this town during the last few months! Why, the Peterson trouble would have ruined the church in a little while. If our minister hadn't had the sense to go directly to Mr. Peterson and demand an explanation of the whole thing, it would have gone on seething and boiling until we should have had an explosion. As it is, there are those who will always believe that something was wrong, somehow, with somebody. Mrs. Marks didn't mean it; she never means anything, and that feature of her case provokes me as much as any. It makes her so invulnerable. She doesn't recognize her own stories. When they come to her afterward, she looks at them as a creation with which she had nothing to do; but she gives them a lift, just as she did this one. With a few such indefatigable helpers as Mrs. Eastman, such a woman can accomplish wonders, and be composed and charitable all the time. Why, Dr. Nellis says some people look at him yet as though he here a dangerous creature, and it was wonderful in Mrs. Decker to endure his presence, all because Mrs. Marks supposed him to be the attending physician when the Deckers lost their child and thought the associations connected with him ought to have been too painful for them to have had anything more to do with him. That was all *she* meant, she told me so, and you know how it grew as it travelled."

"But I think the saddest thing is that story about Mr. Decker. I never understood how that could have even been shadowed by a foundation."

"Is it possible you have never heard? Why, that indefatigable Mrs. Marks exclaimed and 'Oh'd' over his sickness, 'didn't wonder at it,' you know, and then strung half a dozen sentences about something else on to that, as though they belonged, and away it flew. What *she* meant was that she had taken dinner with him a few days before, and he had mixed acids and sweets in such an abominable manner that she had felt sure at the time that no human stomach could endure it! Wasn't that a remarkable beginning for such a terrible conclusion! Why, there was never anybody who believed the atrocious story less than the woman who started it! When I confronted her with it she was utterly dumbfounded!"

"What troubles me is, how is anybody to be safe from such tongues? Why, it wouldn't take more than a half hour to ruin the reputation of any one of us, at that rate."

"I tell you, the *truth* is disagreeable sometimes, but hints, and shrugs, and exclamation points, and lifted eyebrows, and ominous *silences* are infamous. I'd engage to make out a case of murder in the first degree with a few such aids. Mrs. Marks is perfectly adept in their use, and the woman talks in such a virtuous way about the sin of *'gossiping'* that it is enough to drive one distracted. Why, in that regular combat that I had with her, though I was as plainspoken as a mortal could be, I didn't succeed in making her more than half believe that she herself was at fault. To be sure she had an idiotic world to back her, to repeat and increase all she said and interpret her signs to suit their silly selves, but she always *will* have those aids; and she will go right on making mischief and never discover that she is doing it, or recognize her own stories when they are brought to her."

"The woman needs a dose of reconstructed golden rule to digest!" said Mr. Truman, as he folded his napkin. His wife paused in her talk long enough to bestow a puzzled look on him, and at last asked:

"Frank, what do you mean?"

"Why, if she had a taste of 'whatsoever I say about others, even so will they say about me,' it might teach her a wholesome lesson or two."

"Oh, I comprehend. I wish with all my heart she *could* have such a lesson, if it were not too severe; for really the composed way in which she used up Hattie Phillips, because she made her dress too short-waisted, is simply dreadful; and then the most exasperating feature of it is that she actually takes credit to herself for not having told of it; when what she said or rather what she *didn't* say, was infinitely worse."

From this outburst started the talk that developed finally into a plan that was arranged with many bursts of laughter and resulted in the two couples issuing from the Truman mansion in the course of the evening ready to make a social call on Mrs. Marks. As they were intimately acquainted with that lady and occasionally spent an evening with her, their arrival awakened no surprise. The first lull that occurred after the general preliminaries to conversation had been attend to, Mr. Truman, with a peculiar little 'ahem!' that notified the rest of the company to watch for something special, asked if Mr. Marks was expected home soon, and added:

"That is a very disagreeable circumstance connected with his business, isn't it? I was very sorry for him when I heard of it."

Instant alarm overspread Mrs. Marks's face as she eagerly questioned:

"What circumstance?—has anything happened?"

"Oh, nothing new; nothing but what you are well acquainted with, of course. I was only thinking how hard it was for businessmen to weather such troubles. But I hope he will get through all right."

Then Mrs. Watson:

"Mrs. Marks, your daughter Flora has her share of trouble, doesn't she? I really don't see how she bears up under it so well. It is ridiculous to make light of such *peculiar* troubles. But some people have no feeling."

Then Mr. Watson:

"Yes, indeed: I think she is to be pitied; and you, too, Mrs. Marks; a mother suffers so much under such circumstances. It is a wonder that you endure it and look as well as you do."

Then Mrs. Truman:

"And, in view of the *peculiar circumstances* by which you are to be surrounded next week, that, of course, will add to your perplexities. I declare, you have my sympathies."

Each of these sentences had followed each other in such rapid succession that Mrs. Marks, whose face had been growing more and more disturbed and finally frightened, now interrupted Mr. Truman, just as he was commencing with:

"For my part I think Mr. Marks has—" with the eager and anxious exclamation:

"What in the world do you all mean? For mercy's sake, speak out plainly and tell me what you are talking about! I haven't the least idea what has happened. *I* am not in any affliction, nor are my circumstances *peculiar,* so far as I know. You must be insane, or else you know something about my affairs that I do not. Now, what *do* you mean?"

Her answer was peal on peal of laughter, so utterly

uncontrollable and so heartily joined in by each one that it is hardly a wonder that Mrs. Marks's face darkened, not only with perplexity, but with indignation.

"Really," she said began, "this is extraordinary! What am I?"

Mr. Truman interrupted her:

"My dear madam, we ought to beg your pardon for frightening you. But, if you will reflect a moment, what have we said, after all, that should cause you any disturbance? There really has not been a single statement made as *yet,* and our talk may mean anything or nothing, may it not, just as you pleased to interpret it?"

"Is this a practical joke?" asked Mrs. Marks, with an effort to be composed, "or did you come here to insult me?"

Then Mrs. Truman interposed:

"Dear Mrs. Marks, we have no intention of insulting you. We beg your pardon for laughing, but it was funnier than we thought it was going to be. Don't you remember, in the conversation that I had with you a few weeks ago, you declared that no statement which you had made, so far as you could see, was sufficient to have caused anyone trouble, or even anxiety; that you were at perfect liberty to refer to a circumstance, and yet not explain what you were thinking of, if you chose, and no harm could result, unless one were intentionally malicious. To prove to you how mistaken this idea is, we proposed to refer to certain circumstances connected with you—not to a *third party,* you know, but directly to your face—and see what your impression would be. Now, in point of fact, Mr. Truman, in speaking of your husband, refers simply to the heavy loss sustained six months ago, through the failure of Barnes & Burton. It was certainly 'disagreeable,' and businessmen often find it hard to 'weather such troubles.' And that was all Mr. Truman said. And yet, my dear friend, did you get any sort of an idea what he meant?"

"And I," said Mrs. Watson, "meant nothing in the world but the fact that you told me yourself about poor Flora having been kept awake with the tooth-ache every night for a week; if that isn't trouble, I don't know what is. To be sure, I didn't *say* anything about toothache, but then I *meant* that."

"And I meant," said Mr. Watson, "that I didn't see how you bore being broken of your rest so much; and it's a fact, I don't."

Mrs. Truman chimed in again: "And Mrs. Marks, I referred, if you remember, to the 'peculiar circum-stances' by which you are to be surrounded next week. Aren't house painters and two dressmaker's trials enough for one week to merit the term *'peculiar?'* You told me yourself about them, and that is all I meant; but how were you to know it?"

You are to remember that Mrs. Marks was a sensible woman; a woman who *meant* right. To say that she was not indignant to the very verge of endurance with her callers would too faintly express her state of mind; and yet she really had received a lesson such as a week of mere *talking* would not have shown her. It began to dawn upon her that the manner of conversation of this insane party was strikingly like her own, when she felt a desire to give some item of news and yet decided that she would better not; and *yet* could not, or *did* not, resist the temptation to throw a tinge of mystery around her story. She sat looking thoughtfully from one to the other of her guests, reflecting whether she should, in a dignified manner, ask then to be kind enough to retire and leave her in quiet possession of her own house, or own that she was severely and richly rebuked.

They on their part were waiting for the result in no little anxiety; for now that the excitement of the thing was passing they began to realize that it was a severe practical test of her pride, and they were not practical jokers by profession. Indeed, an eager desire to prevent mischief in the future had impelled them. Mrs. Truman had intentionally woven into the plan certain phrases, such as 'peculiar circumstances' and the like, which Mrs. Marks had been in the habit of constantly using. They had been recognized, and almost against her will that woman had been led to go over rapidly certain conversations in which she had indulged.

She realized, as she had never done before, how fraught with meaning her ambiguous phrases might have sounded. All this passed rapidly through her mind, and though her pride was stung to the quick and her indignation was great, she did what was, perhaps, the best thing to be done under the circumstances—she laughed. At the first outburst of this nature her callers joined, and the laugh became full and uncontrolled.

Mrs. Marks's very first words, after the laugh had subsided, were words of wisdom: "'Behold how great a matter a little fire kindleth!'" she said, slowly and thoughtfully.

"'The tongue is a fire, a world of iniquity!'" quoted Mrs. Truman. "How true this it! I tell you our tongues need closer looking after than any other part of us. I feel the force of my own temptation in this direction as I have never done before."

"She bore it splendidly!" said the callers as they trooped home one hour afterward, having eaten apples and nuts in Mrs. Marks's best parlor and departed on better terms with her then they ever had been before, feeling a degree of respect for her that all her prudence, and charity, and foresight had never been able to evolve. For Mrs. Marks had by that first laugh routed Satan, and he slunk away, feeling himself vanquished. Since she *would not* be angry, even under those circumstances, that battle was lost.

"Splendid!" repeated Mr. Truman. "She is a better woman than *I* ever thought her. I'll own up, now, that I never believed her habit of using her tongue to be so free from malicious intent, as it evidently is."

"Nor I," said his wife. "I had serious doubts, and they made me dislike her. I thought even her professions of charity were affectations. But I was evidently mistaken in her. On the whole, I feel meeker tonight than I have in a good while. I guess I have been looking down from a serene height on Mrs. Marks and her clique. But there are more ways than one of entertaining Satan. Now, *I* should have ordered this entire party out of my house and invited them never to come again, if they had talked to me as we did to her tonight."

"'Bear ye one another's burdens, and so fulfill the law of Christ,'" quoted Mr. Truman thoughtfully, as he applied his night key. "A careless use of her tongue is evidently one of Mrs. Marks's burdens, and I guess we ought to have tried to help her, instead of contenting ourselves with criticizing her."

THE END

# PEOPLE WHO HAVEN'T TIME
## AND
## CAN'T AFFORD IT

# 1

## In the Nursery

MRS. Leymon was in the nursery with her sewing; she was nearly always *"with* her sewing." Her needle had almost grown to be a part of herself. She called this pretty, sunny room the nursery, because that was such a pleasant name to her. It suggested the *children's* rights as prominent here; and, besides, if this were not the nursery, then the children had none, and she was bent on their having a spot of their own.

To be sure, the family gathered here for morning prayers and for breakfast; and at dinner time, carts, horses, whistles, slates, and dollies had to be pushed out of the way to make room to set the table, for, in the absence of a dining room, they had to use the nursery. By three o'clock in the afternoon, it was necessary for the little Leymons to gather all the playthings from the four corners of the room, put them away carefully, and get the room in order for chance callers; for the neat and cheery-looking parlor was not a parlor at all, but "Grandma's room," and Grandma wasn't always in the mood to see company. So you perceive that the nursery was also the

Leymons's parlor. It was a useful room, and it bore its part of educating the little Leymons very well, for did they not learn early the necessity for neat and careful disposal of their playthings and their books? Besides, since Mother nearly always sat in the nursery with sewing, there were many helpful little things that they could do for her such as threading needles, finding lost scissors, stray spools, or pins.

In short, because the Leymons were obliged to make a dining, sewing, and sitting room of the nursery, the *little* Leymons were learning to be orderly, helpful, courteous people. Now you know the social *status* of the Leymons, as well as though I had talked of them for hours—people who could not afford to banish the children and sit in elegant idleness in the elegant parlor, waiting for calls.

On the wintry afternoon of which I write, the nursery was at its sunniest. It was a south room and was prettily furnished. There was an easy chair for Freddy Leymon, a dainty rocker for Milly Leymon, and a carved and cushioned highchair for Baby Leymon; it was a notion of this mother to have everything pretty nice and pretty bright for her children, and then to help them take care of it. The mother sat among her children and sewed on a scarlet dress that was neither for Milly, nor yet for baby. In fact, the mother made many dresses and aprons and sacks and waists, and every other bewildering article of the child's toilet, which did not belong to the wardrobe of the little Leymons.

Very early in her life she had discovered that there *were* mothers who *could* not make these pretty garments for their own darlings, and who would pay a fair price to other mothers to make them. So the shining needle flew, and many things were fashioned by her skillful fingers, and many a bright dollar was added to the family purse, for they had all things in common, this couple. Mr. Leymon worked early and late at his machinery, and Mrs. Leymon worked early and late at *her* machinery; though I am willing to admit that she had to reset the gauges and change works oftener than he did.

As she sewed, she thought. Baby Leymon slept the sleep of a healthy, clean, warmly dressed, well-fed baby in her crib in the corner, her eyes shaded from the sun by a screen that the careful papa had made and the careful mamma had covered—slept despite the noise of a train of cars that were just setting off guided by engineer Freddy, and a vigorous rub-a-dub-dub on the washboard as little Miss Milly put Seraphina's clothes through the ordinary processes of a wash. Baby had been taught to sleep on through these and kindred noises, and she did it.

As for Mrs. Leymon, her face was grave and thoughtful, and as often as she looked at or answered the questions of either of her darlings, the shadow of thought on her face deepened. The fact is, but a very few days before, she had unexpectedly come in contact with one of the social problems of our free and independent country, and it puzzled and troubled her.

It had transpired that the little garments were so accumulating on her hands that she found it necessary to look up one of those objects with which her hitherto busy life had little to do, viz., a washerwoman.

She found her, and she also found many other things. She went up and down certain streets where she had never walked before; and she found, dreadful to relate, miserable, half-naked, half-starved children—miserable, neglected, filthy homes—miserable, filthy, sickly, hopeless mothers. What a horrible sight it was! How shall I describe to you Mrs. Leymon's feelings as she thought of *her* home, *her* husband, and *her* children and looked in upon these terrible homes and saw these reeling husbands and these *dreadful* children!

She had heard, indeed, of misery, poverty, hunger, cold, and sickness, in their low and repulsive and altogether horrible forms; but to hear a thing, and *see* it, for the first time, with one's wide-open, startled eyes, are two very different matters. She questioned some of these swarming homes. Did the children go to school? To school! They "had not rags enough to wear at home, let alone school."

"Well, then, surely they went to Sunday school?"

"To Sunday school?" And the answer was intensified with a sneer. "Who would let the likes of *them* into Sunday school?"

"Did they know about Jesus, who came down from heaven to save them?" This last question was asked in a hesitating, awestricken tone, as from one who was almost afraid to speak that dear name in such atmosphere, lest she should indeed be casting pearls before absolute swine, and yet he died even for these. But her answer was a deeper sneer. "Jesus! What was he to such as them, or what did he care what became of them? If he died for them, why did he not give them clothes enough to keep them from freezing, or bread enough to keep them from stealing?"

What could Mrs. Leymon say? What could she *do*? "The poor ye have always with you," she murmured it to her own soul; then they were indeed a God-given trust! What had *she* ever done for the poor? A few cold pieces, now and then, as one of the bolder of them begged at her door; a garment saved up for someone who she knew was struggling with poverty; a dime in the basket occasionally of a Sunday, when a "collection for the poor" was called for. This was the extent of her work for them.

As for sacrifice, she had *heard* of the word, in fact she believed that several times in life it could have been applied to her. Didn't she go without a new dress all one winter, when they were paying for their pretty little cottage? But that was for *herself.* Well, didn't she do without a girl all through the hot summer weather, in order that Freddy and Milly and baby could have two weeks at the seaside? But that was for her *children,* dearer than herself. Well, didn't she get along without a new cloak this very winter, in order to help toward the refurnishing of the church? But that was for herself, and her *husband,* and her *children,* and was to be enjoyed by them for years to come. Was it sacrifice? If she chose a pretty church for herself, instead of a pretty cloak for herself, had she a right to say that she had sacrificed for Christ?

Very solemn questions did Mrs. Leymon ask herself, as, warned by the gathering darkness, she suddenly left the miserable street and went home, sick at heart. Since which time she had done some earnest thinking, which, as she sewed the strawberry buttons onto the scarlet dress, was rapidly settling into fixed resolve. Even before the last one was sewed, she gathered up her work, went swiftly over to Grandma's door, and tapped. It was a dainty courtesy that she was trying to teach the children, this remembrance always to tap at Grandma's door; and of course they could not be expected to do it unless she set the example.

"Would Grandma come and sit with the children, while she went out for a couple of hours?"

"Surely," said a cheery voice from within; and

Grandma's black dress, white hair, white cap, and smiling face beamed lovingly on the little folks. "I'll take the best care of them, and we'll have the nicest of times. I *do* hope you are going out for a little enjoyment this afternoon, and not always business."

Mrs. Leymon smiled. "Yes," she said. "I am going for enjoyment; if I can accomplish what I want, I'm sure I shall enjoy it."

Can you guess what she was after? Do you know that out of her inner consciousness during the week that she had sat and sewed, she had resolved a scheme so broad and deep and far-reaching that it thrilled her; and yet that seemed to her the most reasonable thing to do, and a thing that it was only necessary to mention to the Christian world, to meet with their eager approval and help. Her schemes, as I say, branched in various directions. One of them was a school for the children, in two branches, to teach them to sew, cook, sweep, wash dishes, dust, set table, and oh! well, all sorts of work—not all at once, you know, but gradually, little by little. The sewing school would commence right away, and the other blessings would follow in logical order. Not only the children, but the mothers would be provided with garments for their own wear and taught how to make them, how to take care of their homes, make their beds properly, furnished with proper bedclothing, and shown how to keep it in order. They could be shown how to care for the poor, little, neglected babies that it made her heartsick just to think of; taught how to fill, in short, the place that God designed a woman, a wife, and a mother to fill. I hope you see how wide this beautiful scheme of hers was! And yet you have not glanced at the half of it. There was lying in back of all this, of course, eager plans for the souls, the priceless, never-dying souls that were being dwarfed inside these dreadful bodies and being dragged down by the very force of the physical into absolute shipwreck.

Mrs. Leymon was full of enthusiasm; she was aglow with her subject. She was amazed that she had, meta-phorically, folded her hands and idled away her life so far as the needs of others were concerned. She meant to do it no longer, and she knew, or, bless her innocent heart, she *thought* she knew of hundreds who would join her, with heart and soul and purse. The purse was the part that, for herself, she could not compass, but she reflected with satisfaction that the Lord had many stewards in the First Church to whom he had en-trusted houses and lands, and gold and silver. There was no need for that part of the work to fail. So, behold her arrayed in her winter best, ready for calls on a certain number of families whose names were on the same church roll as her own and who were amply supplied with leisure and wealth. She hoped to make rapid work during those two hours; for she was one, who having little time in which to work, must needs work *fast*.

She made her first attempt in Mrs. Van-Nornam's elegant uptown mansion. Mrs. Van-Nornam was young, bright, and beautiful; having unlimited wealth, and unlimited control over it, and, withal, having the reputation of possessing a very kind heart and warm impulses; and Mrs. Van-Nornam was a Christian. Who so well calculated to give time, money, and enthusiasm to so great a work as this?

The servant eyed Mrs. Leymon's plain black cash-mere and neat cloak of last year's style, somewhat dubiously while he waited for her card, and finally had to ask her name. Before he had received his answer, he had determined her position in society and left her standing in the grand hall, while he went to announce her to his mistress.

Little cared she for that; the hall was grander than any parlor with which she was familiar, and she looked about her with genuine interest, and feasted her beauty loving eyes on its appointments.

She did not hear Mrs. Van-Nornam's half impatient soliloquy; "What on earth can she want? A sewing woman, you think, James?"

"Something of that sort, ma'am, I should say."

"Well, let her come up here; she wants work, I presume."

But Mrs. Leymon's entrance was cordial, and her greeting that of an equal. She had sat in the same pew with Mrs. Van-Nornam at Communion two Sabbaths before and remembered that she was greeting a sister in the Lord. Then she eagerly, with bright eyes, ringing voice, and animated expressions, unfolded her errand, as one who expected to come in contact with an instant heartthrob of sympathy. She was suddenly interrupted:

"My dear woman, do you actually say you went into the creatures' houses and sat down on their horrible chairs? Really, I think it was a tempting of Providence; what horrible diseases you may have brushed against; how could you?"

"But the awful need for somebody to do it, Mrs. Van-Nornam, think of that! I did not come in closer contact than was necessary, and it is to remove such a dreadful state of things that I want your help. And besides," she hurried on, seeing Mrs. Van-Nornam's lips about to open and not liking the expression of her face, "I found some, and indeed they were the saddest cases, who, in their abject poverty, were yet clean and had made pitiful attempts to put their bare homes into something like decency. Such people need help. If we had a room where their children could come once a week, and indeed where *they* could come to get help, to learn ways of managing and get a breath of hope breathed into their discouraged souls, think what a transformation it would soon make in their lives."

"It looks like an utterly wild idea," said Mrs. Van-Nornam, settling back among her cushions and opening wide the book in which she had kept the place with her finger. "A perfectly unpractical and undesirable thing. Whom could you get, who would endure the horrors of spending an afternoon with them? Certainly, no one who had self-respect or who knew enough of *decency* to be able to teach anything, if any of them wanted to learn, which of course they don't."

Two red spots began to glow on Mrs. Leymon's cheeks. "I would spend an afternoon a week, willingly," she said firmly, "and there are *some* things I could teach them."

"You! Well, my good woman, I advise you never to do it. There *must* be less horrible ways of earning a living than that."

Mrs. Leymon rose hastily; she had made a mistake; surely the Lord Jesus Christ could not be this woman's Elder Brother! No hope of *her* devoting of her leisure to help his poor up to a knowledge of him! Yet there were her hundreds of thousands. *Could* she go away without enlisting some little mite from them for the treasury of her Lord? She kept down her indignation, and was meek. "If you cannot give this matter your personal help, will you not lead my paper with a subscription that shall start the thought for others?"

Mrs. Van-Nornam hesitated, opened her tiny jeweled watch, started with an air of well-bred surprise at the lateness of the hour, rang her bell, gave an order to the servant to the effect that her carriage should be ready precisely at four, then turned again to her caller. "I really haven't time to investigate the matter this evening; some day I will look into it, perhaps, and determine whether to give you a donation, though, as I told you, it doesn't commend itself to my judgment. I think it will be, very likely, money thrown away, and for yourself, I don't believe you would find it profitable employment." Then she settled back to her cushions and her book!

Then Mrs. Leymon went with speed and resolved on her way downstairs that she would never, no, *never*, ask that woman for money again. Let us hope that she broke that foolish resolution.

# 2

✦━❧❦❧━✦

## Making Calls

HER next stop was at Mrs. Jarvis Veeder's mansion. Mrs. Veeder was not in, but the young ladies were. "Would she see the young ladies?" Yes, she would; they were graduated young ladies, having "finished their education," whatever that may mean. They certainly ought to have a degree of leisure, and if their father could be induced to help along an industrial school with his money, perhaps they would help it with their time and their education.

She was shown to the back parlor where were the Misses Veeder, and with them two other young ladies, each with their fancy work.

They gave her kindly greeting; she was a frequent caller at the house, for she made lovely dresses and aprons for the little Veeders.

I wish I could give you a glimpse of that back parlor! It was a most luxurious room. Wealth and taste and skill had united in making it a place of beauty. If it had a fault, it was that it was crowded. Especially Mrs. Leymon's eyes rested curiously on the number of fancy ornaments which filled the available spaces;

tidies of every hue and shape and design on the backs of rockers and easy camp chairs, and on the three-cornered sofa three of them, three on the *tete-a-tete,* and on the arms of all the chairs that could boast of arms.

The vases, on mantles and brackets, rested on mats of bright-colored wools, rose mats and pansy mats and tulip mats, and every grade and shape of mat seemed literally to swarm. Worsted cats curled composedly in the corners of the hassocks with which the room was plentifully supplied. In front of the doors were elegant mats of rich design, a great, gray woolly dog occupying one center, heavily surrounded with fine worsted work, known to the initiated by the name of "filling in." At the other door was one of those devices of Satan for consuming time and money—an elegant mat manufactured out of ravelled Brussels carpeting laboriously knit together again; and a sleeping lion in wools and beads crouched in the center of the hearth rug.

In short, the menagerie, in green and blue and yellow and brown wools, that curled in millennial peace together in that room represented a small fortune in money and an almost unlimited number of hours.

And, wonderful to relate, all these works of art were the product of the united skill of the young ladies of the house. Mrs. Leymon had long been aware of this fact, for the fond mother loved to boast of her daughters' "industry." Surely, having done up the fancywork for a century to come, these young ladies were the ones to devote their leisure to industrial schools. She explained the subject with equal clearness, but with not quite the enthusiasm that she had shown at Mrs. Van-Nornams. That lady had had a quieting effect on her ardor.

"Well," said Miss Lilian Veeder, "I'm sure it is a nice idea; real sweet of you to think of it, Mrs. Leymon. But who will be the teachers? You say you will need a good many; where are they to come from?"

"Why," said wily Mrs. Leymon, "it must be a benevolent work entirely, of course; so we must depend mainly on those who have their time at their own disposal. I thought perhaps you and your sister would take up the work."

"My patience!" said Miss Lilian. And "The idea!" said Miss Evelyn. "Why, Mrs. Leymon, I hope you don't think we are ladies of leisure! I assure you, I am hurried from morning till night. Last Christmas I sat up until midnight two or three times to finish my bead cushion; and I have at least a dozen pieces of fancywork in the house this minute waiting to be finished. When they ever *will* be, I'm sure I don't know. You see, Mrs. Leymon, we have such a host of friends, and they all expect something in the fancy line from us, knowing that we understand all such work, and that our large house requires so much of that sort. Oh, dear me! don't mention *our* doing anything of the kind. I'm sure I shudder at the thought of the holidays, or of weddings, or of people's birthdays, for fear I shall be so crowded with work."

And Miss Lilian sighed and pushed back her hair from her flushed forehead and bent over her white silk Spitz dog and said, "One, two, three, four. No. Why, one, two, three. There! I've made a mistake! Now, that dog's nose will all have to be taken out! What a shame! I declare I won't speak again in an hour."

As for Miss Evelyn, she had exhausted the time at her disposal in the sublime sentence, "The idea!" and from that time had devoted herself most energetically to her bead fringes, keeping up an incessant murmur-

ing of "one, two, three, purl; one, two, three, purl," till
you wondered that she didn't scream over the stupid-
ity of the thing. It was impossible not to measure the
amount of mental and physical *and spiritual* life of
these two young ladies by a comprehension of their
absorptions. Mrs. Leymon, without suffering herself
to waste any arguments at all on them, turned to their
friends, Miss Alice Markham and Miss Margie Lee,
both of them members of the same church with
herself; both of them pledged not to live for themselves, but for Christ; both of them with fathers whose
bank accounts supplied all their wants, real and fancy;
both of them having graduated at Madame De Long's
Seminary. How did these young ladies occupy their
time? She appealed to them. Miss Alice answered with
spirit:

"I've always observed, Mrs. Leymon, that you
people who are very industrious suppose that young
ladies who do not have to work for a living have
therefore nothing to do. Now, certainly, *I* am not a
young lady of leisure. I am keeping up my music; I
practice four hours a day! That in itself consumes
about all the available time between calls and going
out. And then I read French and German as regularly
as I did in school. An industrial school may be a very
good idea, though probably about the last thing that
these dreadful people want is to be industrious. Why
don't they go to work? That is what I always wonder.
There is a great deal of useless sympathy wasted on
the poor, miserable set."

"But the children," ventured Mrs. Leymon, who
realized that to attempt argument with this lady
would be a literal casting of pearls where they would
not be appreciated.

"Well, the children—lazy, thieving set! Just as bad as

they *can* be. The little boys who come from the Higby Lane region are a disgrace to the city; and as for the girls, Miss Maurice has been trying to gather some of them into her mission class—actually *coaxed* the little wretches to come, bribed them with sugarplums, and how did they repay her—one of them stole her pencilcase the very first Sunday! And they looked more like animals than human beings. And smelled! Faugh!"

Words failed Miss Alice, and Mrs. Leymon turned from her promptly. A young lady who could bring forward the utter degradation of the poor as a reason for doing nothing for them was *not* the material needed for teachers in an industrial school. But before she left her, she could not resist the temptation to ask one question, which she meant as a probe to that lady's conscience.

"May I ask you, Miss Markham, what you are going to do with your music and French and German?"

"Do with them?" queried Miss Markham, in a half wondering, half supercilious tone. "Why, my good woman, what do people generally do with talents and superior education?"

"That is a solemn question," said Mrs. Leymon. "It really needs to be settled on one's knees before the Lord. If music, French, and German are worthy of the absolute absorption of all our available time, to the exclusion of any other of God's work, then, if we are Christians, they must in some way be doing God's work, else we are not applying our talents to the end that they were given, nor to the end that we covenanted when we united with his visible church. I am simply asking for information, Miss Markham. I suppose, of course, your special talents are consecrated."

Then she turned entirely from her and looked at Miss Lee.

Are you interested to know what that young lady was engaged in—an occupation which so absorbed her that apparently she had neither eyes, nor ears, for any other earthly object? She was snipping holes in a piece of cloth, and sewing them up again! Snipping carefully, skillfully, sewing them with infinite pains and millions of delicate stitches, requiring patience and skill. She called them "wheels," and "eyelets," and "leaves," and "scollops," and when they were done it was *"perfectly exquisite"* and was designed for the infantile robe of an atom of humanity, who luxuriated in more of that article now than her weary overburdened little body knew how to bear up under. The maker of the said embroidery was civil and ladylike; she smiled kindly on Mrs. Leymon, "hoped she would succeed." Such things were needed, she supposed, though *she* never had time to think much about it. She was always busy—one thing and another took up the time, until now she really was busier than she had been when in school. She never could teach *anybody;* sewing, and lessons, and all that, she had no taste for; had tried to teach her own little sister to hem and made wretched work of it. Still, there must be people who had time for such things, people on whom society didn't make so many demands. They were just the ones, too, for they could understand the poor, enter into their feelings, as, of course, people of position and culture couldn't be expected to do.

"But after all," said Mrs. Leymon, "the one who seemed to understand the poor better than any other person who ever lived was the Lord Jesus Christ." And then, in a moment, she was sorry that she had said it, for these young ladies all looked at her as though she had someway said an improper thing; for aught she knew, they would not have considered Jesus of Nazareth a person of position and culture!

But she left them to their dogs, cats, fringes, and snippings and betook herself to the next name on her list, Mr. E. D. Landor. This family were at dinner, and she was ushered cordially to the dining room.

"Come in, come in," said Mr. Landor heartily. He was a merchant and the stockholder in half a dozen factories, and everybody spoke of him as a whole-souled, generous-hearted man. "Come right in. Have some dinner with us? You have dined, eh? Sensible woman to dine at a reasonable hour. Ah well, and how is your good husband, the best machinist that comes about my premises? He will make his fortune yet, and deserves to."

All this Mr. Landor said in a brisk business tone, carrying on his eating at the same time, with rapidity and skill. He was used to giving attention to several important affairs at once. Mrs. Leymon took courage from his cheery voice and loud cheery manner and unfolded her errand.

I grieve to tell you that the benevolent face settled into an ominous frown. "Now, my good friend, you are dealing in a kind of filth that won't wash off. Let me advise you as a sensible woman to let that sort of scum alone. It is all stuff to talk about the *worthy* poor. There is no such thing. It is a crime to be poor in this country; a man ought to be punished for it."

"Mr. Landor," said Mrs. Leymon with spirit, "now you are talking nonsense, and you know you are. Any man who calls himself a patriot and remembers the army of soldiers who came home from the war ruined in health and crippled in limbs, has no right to say any such thing. I had a friend who went, and who *came,* and who is poor, dependent on others for his support. Now!"

"Well, well," said Mr. Landor. "There are exceptions, of course, but they only prove the rule. The masses of the poor are so because they have been improvident, extravagant, dissipated, idle, everything that is mean, and to be condemned. I have no patience with their whining, beggarly ways, nor with schemes for lifting them up. They have been lifted up too much; they need letting down. They ought to be sent to State's Prison, every one of 'em."

# 3

## VARIED EXPERIENCES

"AND their children, too, I suppose."

"And their children to the House of Correction, or any other place where they can be kept from being a pest to the city. Those are my sentiments, and you are welcome to them."

And Mr. Landor brought his hand down on the table in so emphatic a manner that the plate glass shivered at the jar, and he thereby evinced that this was a sore question with him, touching somewhere a bare spot in his conscience. As for Mrs. Leymon, his excitement seemed to cool and quiet her.

"You are more willing to support the poor than I supposed," she said with quiet sarcasm in voice and manner. "I certainly do not expect any such munificent donation as you will have to give, for your share, if you propose to have this great army of people clothed and fed for the future at the expense of the State. Now, *I* was for putting them in a way to help themselves, but you propose to take care of them and their children for all time. Still, there is one trouble in the way—what about their souls? The prisons and penitentiaries stand ready, I suppose, to look after their bodies; at least *you* can be taxed to help build places large enough to receive them, but will they assume the responsibility of the souls? I thought the Lord left that work for us, his professed followers. He said they would be always with us. He didn't say anything about our finding them nowhere save in prisons and penitentiaries."

Mr. Landor stared at her as though she were talking in an unknown tongue.

"The fact is," he said after a moment, "I haven't time to be sentimental about this thing. I have had to work hard myself; am working hard yet; and I am not given to gush or sentiment of any sort. A man like your husband, who can work for his wages, I am willing to respect; but a man who comes sniveling around me expecting sympathy because he doesn't want to work and support his family, I've neither time nor patience for. *I can't* afford to support the poor of this city, Mrs. Leymon.

"In point of fact, now, what do you want to do? Have 'soup houses,' and 'free lunches,' and 'hot coffee and sandwiches,' and 'educate the people,' and 'elevate the masses'? I know the terms, you see. All bosh, the whole of it, if you'll excuse my saying so. And your husband is much too sensible a man to allow you to get mixed up with it, or I'm mistaken. As long as you feed the vagrants for nothing, they will be willing to be fed; and as long as they can live without work, they'll do it. As for the children who are too young to work, they have got to suffer for the sin of their parents. That's Bible. I'll risk any of them starving, either; that sort never do. No, ma'am, I can't head your list; can't afford it. Let 'em work and earn their living as I do."

Mrs. Leymon arose to go. Long ago she had decided that this man could not claim brotherhood with the self-sacrificing, long-suffering Lord. She began to feel that his family on earth was smaller than she had supposed. Yet her voice was not disheartened, nor her manner that of one crushed.

"Well, Mr. Landor, we shall have an industrial school, and try to teach these children to work and earn their own living; and we shall have soup houses, too, by and by, and sandwiches and coffee, and when you come to lunch with us *you* shall not be insulted by being offered anything *free!* You shall pay a good round price for it. I am sorry that you don't see the way clear to help us, but we shall do it."

She did not know in the least who the "we" meant, but the Lord knew. He honored her faith, just then, with a touch of sight.

"Uncle Frank"—a clear, youthful voice came up from the lower end of the table—*"I* want to help about this thing. Madam, if you please, I will head your list. I can't do it so well as my uncle could, if he would; but almost anybody can *start* a thing." And she reached forth her hand for the paper. "I'll write my subscription in pencil, and, in order to be sure that it is binding, you may, if you please, pay it now, Uncle Frank."

"But, my dear child, you should take time to reflect before you waste your money."

"I *have* reflected—long enough to know that somebody may be starving just this minute! I'll help feed them first and reflect afterward."

"But, Maude, I am your guardian, remember. I don't know that I ought to let you waste your money."

She pushed the paper toward him, with a gleam in her eye that meant business, as she said:

"But, Uncle, I am of age, remember. If I choose to waste my money, I am not sure that you can help it."

A flush of victory mounted to Mrs. Leymon's very forehead as she received back her subscription paper, and she gave her hand to the young girl with an eager "Thank you!" that was almost like a benediction. She saw the clear, unmistakable characters that had been traced on the paper: "Maude L. Harlowe, one hundred dollars."

"I want to be one of your teachers," Miss Maude said earnestly, retaining the hand and looking with strong, grave eyes into Mrs. Leymon's liquid ones. "That is, if you will teach me how. I don't know anything about such work, but I know I can learn."

"Maude!" in harsh tones from her uncle. "Why, Maudie!" in pleading ones from her aunt. "My dear child, I wouldn't have you do such a thing for the world! Such a horrid place for infection!"

Miss Maude laughed.

"My life is no more precious than others, Auntie. If you are afraid to have me board here, I'll go to the Sansom House. They are not afraid of any amount of infection, if you give them money enough. Anyway, I'm going to work in this school if I can get a chance. Uncle Frank, there is no use in talking; I know what I am about. My father got the first dinner he had had for three days in a public soup house once, and you began your education in a charity school, you know. Do you think I could forget the debt of gratitude I owe?"

Was Mrs. Leymon discouraged with her two hours' work, do you think? Not a bit of it! She was not the woman to have gone home discouraged and to have folded her hands and wept over failure, even had she not met Miss Maude Harlowe that afternoon. Indeed,

I will own that she was of the temperament which made her, after the third rebuff, set her lips together in the firm way that some women can, and say to herself: "Now we *will* have an industrial school, and all the other improvements." But then, meeting Miss Maude, having her name on a bit of paper, hearing her words, and clasping her hand made her feel gloriously triumphant; made her feel as though she had been at court and clasped hands with one of the princesses of the realm. So, indeed, she had.

She gave an account of her afternoon's work at the tea table—after the little Leymons were sleeping the sleep of downright weariness—detailing her experiences with touches of humor that made the husband shout with laughter and the white strings of Grandma's cap quiver, as she more quietly enjoyed the fun. Then she said:

"You went too far to the other extreme, Daughter; it isn't the *very* rich who can understand and help the very poor—that is, as a rule. There are Miss Maudes, thank the Lord, who are exceptions, but as a *rule* the busy workers are the ones to join heart and hand in such work."

Mindful of that bit of advice from her wise old mother, Mrs. Leymon, on her very next afternoon of leisure, went out to call on Mrs. Jenny Johnson, who lived in a pretty house just around the corner from the avenue—she being one of those who, though not by any means poor, was certainly not among the wealthy. Mrs. Leymon knew her very well; in fact, exchanged calls with her occasionally. A most unlucky time had she chosen, however, for this call. Mrs. Johnson was preparing for a tea party. She had invited Mrs. Dr. Merchant and Mrs. Judge Butler to take tea with her, as well as a dozen other persons less notable. She was making special preparations. Mrs. Leymon, by virtue of her being an acquaintance and by virtue of the hostess being in great haste and anxiety concerning something in the oven, was suddenly summoned to the dining room to "look at the table" for the feast was to be that very evening. It was worthy of being looked at as a matter of curiosity, if one looked from no other standpoint.

"Having only one girl," explained Mrs. Johnson, as she wiped a streak of flour from her flushed cheek, "makes it necessary for me to set the table before any of them come and obliges me to do the whole of the getting ready myself. I declare, it makes slavish work of having company. If I weren't ashamed about having so many people invite me and never returning it, I don't believe I'd ever get at it in the world. As it is, I haven't invited half the people I wanted. Now, we wanted you and Mr. Leymon tonight, but, dear me, we didn't get around to your street at all."

Mrs. Leymon disclaimed, as best she could, any expectation of an invitation, and then she regarded the table with an amused air, while the overtasked martyr continued her tale of woe.

"I have had to do every bit of the baking myself; and my fruit cake did act abominably; I had to make the second batch before it looked black enough to suit me. My poundcake looks nice, doesn't it? And I had real good luck with my gold, and silver, and orange cakes; but the thing I pride myself on is this lemon cream cake. I do think lemon cream cake is the very prettiest looking cake that ever was made. But such a sight of work as it is! My bones fairly ached the day I made it. I whipped the eggs myself. An eggbeater is nowhere when you come to such delicate work as that."

"Two, three, four, six," counted Mrs. Leymon to herself and smiled again. Six kinds of cake with which to entertain a company of ordinarily well-fed people, after seven o'clock in the evening! Besides, there were pickled pears, pickled plums, currant jelly, grape jelly, canned quince, canned peach, stewed cranberries, chicken salad, cold turkey, as well as oysters scalloping in the oven, as fast as they could.

Poor Mrs. Johnson didn't know that Mrs. Judge Butler, whom she was so anxious to honor, would not have had one half of these dishes at her table; but Mrs. Leymon, who had originally come from an aristocratic tree, was quite aware of it. She wondered within her earnest soul why good sense, or failing in that, why conscience itself did not loudly protest against this foolish waste of money, time, and strength. Mrs. Johnson, in her anxiety, had no room for conscience.

"Do you suppose the cake will dry?" she asked anxiously. "It isn't cut; but I didn't know how to manage unless I had it on the table before they came. I haven't a girl who can attend to any such thing; mine is only a cheap girl. It is one of the miseries of being poor!"

*Poor,* and the mistress of that table, spread for one evening's feast, and not by any means intended for the halt, or the lame, or the blind, or the poor and needy in any form. The word suggested to Mrs. Leymon the object of her call; and more, it must be confessed, because of a curious desire to study human nature from this standpoint than because she had any expectation of help, she made known her wants.

# 4

## SOCIETY MARTYRS

"BLESS your heart and soul," exclaimed Mrs. Johnson, dropping now in utter exhaustion on the chair behind her. "*I've* neither time nor money for anything. I'm harassed to death now with all that I have to do. I work like a slave, Mrs. Leymon, I really do. Every bit of my baking I have to do myself; cakes, and pies, and puddings, and getting fruits ready, all such things I have to attend to. It is just work, *work,* from morning till night. Mercy knows I'm sorry for the poor, if anybody is; but as for giving an afternoon a week to them, I couldn't do it any more than I could fly! I just get through now, and that is all. I haven't time to read more than if I couldn't, and Sundays I'm so tired I just lie and doze half the time. I'd help if I could, and I hope you'll succeed; but I've got a large family to take care of, you know, and they are hearty eaters. Mr. Johnson thinks as much of his pies and puddings as he does of me, and I'm the only one who can make them to suit him. Dear me! I haven't time to do anything! And, as for money, my! What little I get of it, I could use a dozen ways at once anytime. Actually,

I have to spend a good deal of time in planning what we can do *without* the longest. Oh, I know what it is to be poor. I tell you, I'm sorry for them."

And six kinds of cake on her supper table! was Mrs. Leymon's mental comment. Then she thought of the poor people whom she had visited that week and contrasted their homes with Mrs. Johnson's. But that lady was in a hurry; her oysters were overdoing, and her toilet was not quite made, and it was growing late. There was no use to talk to her. Yet Mrs. Leymon by no means despaired of her; she knew an argument that is often needed for such natures as hers, as well as for some natures not in the least like hers.

"I tell you what it is, Mrs. Johnson," she said briskly. "I mustn't hinder you now, and I hope you will have a real pleasant time this evening. But I want you to promise me that some day next week you will take an afternoon and make some calls with me down on Higby Lane. It will only be one afternoon, you know, and that will help a good deal."

Mrs. Johnson mopped her hot and tired face with her apron and said doubtfully, she didn't know; maybe she could manage to find one afternoon, but she had a great deal to do; still, *one* afternoon, if that would be any help, she would really try to go, after she got rested.

"I'm so tired now," she said frankly, "that if they should all send word they couldn't come, and I could go to bed right away, and sleep till day after tomorrow, I think I should like it best of anything. I never have time to get rested. But *one afternoon*—well, yes, I'll try to do that much."

Mrs. Leymon went away smiling. What homes she would show her!—homes of which she did not dream. What if it should waken her to a sense of her opportunities and *responsibilities?* What if it should even, in time, show her that six kinds of cake made by a woman who has no *time* to do any of Christ's work were six absolute sins? What an accomplishment that would be! And she tripped up the steps to Mrs. Porter's as though she had received a twenty-dollar donation at the last place and expected as much here.

Mrs. Porter was sewing, and she was in her back sitting room, and she had her two children with her. Another Mrs. Leymon's you think. See if it is. That back sitting room was the dingiest spot in the house, and every broken-down piece of furniture that the house contained seemed to have been moved in there.

"I don't make company of you, you see," the hostess said half apologetically, as Mrs. Leymon helped herself to a seat. "The children smash things around so that I don't try to keep anything decent in this room."

She was grim and severe over the question of the poor. She didn't believe in them any more than Mr. Landor did, in a quieter but an equally dogged way.

"I haven't time to go racing up and down the world tending to other folks' affairs," she said severely. "Even if there was need for anybody to do it, I couldn't. People who have to do their own work, sewing and all, are not the ones to look after other folks. I do every stitch of my family's sewing, Mrs. Leymon, and it keeps me slaving night and day."

She was "slaving" at that moment on a polonaise for her daughter Helen, aged twelve; and it had a row of knife pleating all around the bottom, and a row of bows up and down the front, and a row of buttons everywhere! At least so it seemed to Mrs. Leymon's eyes as she surveyed the gleaming things that went over the left shoulder in little clusters as though to have them an inch apart would not have consumed enough of them.

"Why don't those people go to work and earn their own living?"

"Who would employ them, Mrs. Porter? Would you?"

"I? No!" with grim satisfaction, "but there are people enough who like to get their work done for them, while they run around and attend to other folks. I never was one of that sort."

"And in objection to your theory of work, there are a great many *other* people who do their own; some who are obliged to, and some who prefer to, on the score of economy, they think, but really because by so doing they can save enough to be able to put another ruffle on their dress."

Did Mrs. Leymon glance surreptitiously at the skirt which belonged to the polonaise lying near her on a chair, and which had two carefully made and carefully trimmed ruffles on it? Possibly the suggestion that she might have done so made Mrs. Porter savage.

"That's *their* concern, I take it," she said stoutly; "if they choose to spend their money in ruffles, and don't steal, nor beg them, they are accountable to nobody, as I look at it."

"In which we should differ," Mrs. Leymon said, speaking very gently. "You and I have proclaimed before a watching world that *we* are the Lord's; that our time and money and strength and talents belong to him, to do with as *he* directs. Whether, therefore, the time shall be spent in pleating ruffles, and the money in furnishing them, would depend on whether he saw an end to be attained that would honor him, would it not?"

This was new ground to Mrs. Porter. Evidently she

had never realized in her life that she had promised any such thing. Rather, she had plumed herself on being independent. Some answer must be made to this waiting woman, and, puzzled and annoyed, she knew not what to say. It was this that made her voice more irritable in its tone than before.

"I never have time for philosophizing over things; my work always lies before my eyes, and I go ahead and do it the best I can. That's my duty, *I* believe."

"Yes," Mrs. Leymon said, still very gently, "but I think it is one of the most intensely practical questions of the day, and one that I should think would puzzle people more and more, the higher they reach in the social scale—how far their planning and spending and sewing could be made to serve the interests of the Master. But we are not getting on with the question at hand, as to these poor people supporting themselves. Many of them could work if they had the opportunity; but for the women, especially, work is hard to find, and skilled laborers are plenty. And among the men, alcohol, their awful enemy, that a free and intelligent and Christian people have licensed to do its worst, is working wonders of poverty and sin. Then there *are* those who could not work if there were anything for them to do; they are too old, or too sick, or they have little children—swarms of them—clinging to their skirts. Something must be done to save them, or they and their children will go to ruin together."

Mrs. Porter shut her lips tight and sewed and talked fast. "They are a shiftless, drinking, thieving set, the most of them. I know those Higby Lane folks; the very worst scum you can find in the city."

"That is most painfully true; but you know the Bible doesn't read; 'Feed the hungry who are worthy;

clothe the naked who are sober and virtuous; tell the respectable and moral people about Christ and heaven.' You see, Mrs. Porter, these are questions with which, in a sense, we have nothing to do; or, rather, the poorer and lower people are, the more imperative is their need of Christ, who came to save, 'to the uttermost.'"

This time Mrs. Porter sewed away very fast and spoke no word.

"Won't you give us a little of your *time?*" the pleader asked timidly, after a moment of silence. She had not deemed it wise to ask here for money, not that there was no money, but that there were many ruffles and side pleatings and bias bands of silk and velvet, and whatever other costly material was the prevailing fashion; for there was a grown-up daughter, as well as the two little ones and the twelve-year-old.

"I have no *time* to give," was the short and comprehensive answer. "A woman who does her own sewing has dreadful little time, especially if she does her *work* as she ought to do it; and I calculate to keep my house in order. Some folks think that amounts to nothing, but I consider it as much a Christian duty as anything is."

"So do I. I quite long for the privilege of helping some of those poor mothers whom I have been visiting to make their dreary, and in every way dreadful, homes, into something more worthy of the name. How much you could help some of them by a few kind suggestions."

"Well, my own home needs me; I look after that, without any suggestions from anybody, and so might they, I dare say, if they wanted to. It is the desire to do better that's lacking; you may depend upon that. I think my first duty is to my children; I stay at home with them. Who is to look after *my* children, I wonder, while I go to Higby Lane and take care of other people's? Sarah Jane, don't you put your feet on that table again; if you do I'll whip you as sure as you're alive! And, you, Thomas, no more whistling; I'll tell your father on *you;* see if I don't, and then you'll catch it. No, Mrs. Leymon, you and I shouldn't agree, I suppose, if we should talk till midnight. You believe in making homes pleasant for other folks, and I believe in tending to my own home. Sarah Jane, sit down in that chair and don't get up again till I tell you you may. And that's just the difference between us."

By this time Mrs. Leymon was fully of the opinion that she and her neighbor would never agree, even though they talked on forever; and without promise, or shadow of promise or help or sympathy from this Christian woman, she was obliged to take her leave.

At another time, perhaps, Mrs. Porter would not have been so hard-hearted; in truth, she was sore-hearted; she had had a reasonable degree of expectation that she would be invited to partake of those six kinds of cake, and pickles, and cream salad, and hot rolls gotten up by Mrs. Johnson; and not having been summoned to the feast, she was feeling aggrieved thereat. So Mrs. Johnson's duty to society was productive of bitterness in the heart of at least *one* sister, and reacted in a manner that was *not* for the good of the cause.

# 5

## FIRSTFRUITS

WAS Mrs. Leymon discouraged, now, do you think? You must constantly remember that she was not made of the material which discourages, else she would never have started. She counted the cost before ever she *did* start, and assuredly, having put her hand to the plow, she meant not to look back.

She rehearsed her afternoon's work again at the tea table; this time, with more pity and commiseration for the narrow souls of others than with laughter, and Grandma sagely remarked that she hadn't hit the right medium yet. It was not among the people who were engaged in that most hopeless of all struggles, the trying to *seem* rich, that you found open hearts for the needs, and pity for the sins of the abject poor.

Were all the people in Mrs. Leymon's reach of the stamp who ignored their relationship to the souls for whom Christ died? By no manner of means were they! You have only the result of two afternoon of work; and even in those afternoons was there not a Miss Maude, with her golden purse, her fresh young hands, and her consecrated heart? What a glorious helper she was! How they planned and worked together, those two sisters in Christ, revealing, by their loving friendship and cooperation, the very depth of the meaning of that tender and constantly abused term—*sisters in Christ.*

I wish I had time to tell you about other calls and other helpers. Very different some of them from Miss Maude and yet equally grand in their way. There was a mother who had a drunken son, who, with his wife, had gone down into the depths, and the mother, in her neat home, with her widow's weeds and her poverty, wrung Mrs. Leymon's hand and said, 'mid choking tears:

"God bless you! I am doing what I can, but it is very little; and it will be *so* blessed to have help, and God will bless you. He will in very deed."

And Mrs. Leymon, looking at *her,* believed it.

There was crisp, trim little Miss Priscilla Hunter, who sewed all day in her attic room on clothes for boys too young or too poor to go to the regular clothing establishments. Poor was Miss Hunter; that is, people looking on called her so. But, after all, I hardly knew of a richer person than Miss Priscilla Hunter.

"Time!" she said, "bless you, yes; there is always time for what ought to be done, whether it is to finish a jacket or pick up a basket of chips for somebody poorer or lamer than you are yourself. It's a good idea, too. I wonder you have been so many years in getting it thought out. Help! Of course I will. I'll bring my scissors and snip out things for you in odd hours. Oceans of things can be done in odd hours; and I've got a little bundle laid away that will do to make over for somebody; and Mrs. Jackson has an attic full of trumpery that she will never use. I'll see that a good load of it gets sent around to the room. You've got a good room? It's Mr. Hoardwell's, isn't it! Of course he'll let you have it; I'll see him if you want me to; he's a friend of mine. I'll slip up there between daylight and dark and see about it."

What a helper was Miss Priscilla, with her "snipping" and her "slipping" here and there, and her strong, vigorous, helpful words, like whiffs of breezes blowing fresh from off the sea! There was Mrs. Harland, an invalid, never moving out of that one room, never moving in that room, except in her wheeled chair. What wonders she could do! She had access to her husband's purse, through his heart. It was not a very powerful purse, and yet it constantly overflowed toward the Industrial School—for I hope you understand that there *was* an Industrial School, and a soup room, and a free lunch room, or what was better than free, a lunch room where the honest and industrious poor could come, and for five cents purchase a dinner. There were mothers who work, could and did work hard till noon over the washtub, and then slipped around the corner to the depot of supplies, and for a dime purchased food enough for a decent and wholesome dinner for husband and children, ready cooked, when her work made it a necessity to be so prepared. Ready to be cooked, and with careful directions how to cook it, when that was all the help needed. Thus far had broadened and deepened the scheme that had begun in Mrs. Leymon's brain. Further than that, it was taking on new plans and schemes every day. It involved a reading room and a free library open to the poorest, and a store of supplies that could be purchased at the *bare* cost of furnishing them; and, when needful, *less* than the bare cost. It took in a pledge to attend a Sunday school and a church service, and a pledge to neither touch, taste, nor handle anything that could intoxicate. Slowly, but surely, all these plans moved; there was no thought of failure. "Where there is a will there is a way." Dr. Vincent has improved upon that time-honored saying by adding, "Where there is a *woman* there is a *will*."

Grand hearts and great purses took hold of Mrs. Leymon's idea. There was Mr. McMartin, who, as soon as he became aware of what was being attempted, and before it had taken such proportions as to rouse the public pride, inquired and listened and nodded and wrote his check for five hundred dollars and sent it by his errand boy to Mrs. Leymon with his compliments. There was Mrs. Chester, a woman with five children and a sick husband, who sent, tied up in the corner of a handkerchief, a dime for her husband and a dime for herself, and a five-cent piece for each of the five, and an ill-spelled note to the effect that the children prayed every night that God would bless the work. And Mrs. Leymon laid the sacred dimes and five-cent bits side by side with the five-hundred-dollar check and thanked God for them all and knew that in his hands the one could accomplish as much as the other. She had her triumphs, too, as the days went on. The Misses Veeder attired themselves once of a sunny afternoon in summer silks and swept into the Industrial Schoolrooms and "Oh'd!" over the extreme neatness of the little pupils and the skill they had acquired with their needles, and asked:

"Wouldn't it be nice to teach some of them to do fancy work, and they might be able to actually support themselves by it."

And Mrs. Leymon, the superintendent of the enterprise, rejoicing that the young ladies actually desired to consecrate their talents to usefulness, formed a class in fancy needle work, and the young ladies took turns in attending it.

Then came, one day, Mrs. Van-Nornam's carriage, Mrs. Van-Nornam's footman, and a basket of the most elegant frosted plum cakes, in delicate patty tins with Mrs. Van-Nornam's compliments, for the children of the Industrial School, "she was *so* delighted with their singing, the other evening, at the hall."

As for Mrs. Johnson, she had devoted that afternoon to making calls with Mrs. Leymon, and the sights she saw made her so sick at heart and so sore of conscience that she could eat no cake for her supper. At intervals, for several days afterward, she said. "Oh, my!" "Oh, mercy me!" "Dear! dear!" "Who *could* have thought it!" and any other term that seemed to her to express indignation or commiseration or *dismay.* Then she went to work, hands and heart and soul, for the poor. She hasn't given a tea party since that time. Company she has had; pleasant, reasonable gatherings, social reunions in her pretty parlor; but not a single regularly planned, six-caked, pickled, creamed, jellied campaign since that memorable afternoon. She hasn't *"had time!"*

Now there are those who criticize Mrs. Leymon and others of her class. They broadly hint that a woman who has so much to do for others *must* neglect her own; that her house must suffer, or *her* table, or her children, or her dress—*something* is wrong. To be sure, her house is still the sunny home it always was; to be sure, her friends still like to go to Mrs. Leymon's, because "everything always looks so fresh and nice, and the children are so well behaved and happy." But then, of course, something *must be wrong,* or she, with her three children, could never give a whole afternoon each week, to say nothing of constant odd hours, to outside work. It does necessitate care—the husbanding of the seconds, the cutting off of many a ruffle and tuck and frill and pucker. Mrs. Leymon has chosen between them. Since she cannot do both, she has decided that the souls of the poor, whom Satan hath bound, are of more importance than the decorations of the bodies which belong to the Lord's freemen. Was she *above* criticism? Yes, really and truly above it. She had gotten where it hardly jarred—up "on deck"—where the sky was fair. Occasionally she laughed about the comments in a good-natured way. There were always those who stood ready to let her hear of the *comments,* just for friendship's sake, you know. There always will be that class of people on the earth, at least, until the Millennium.

"I really believe I ought to make a tidy," she said briskly to Grandma one evening.

"A tidy!" said Grandma, lifting her head, putting her spectacles up on her forehead, and looking as though she thought much planning had made her daughter mad. "What *does* the child mean?"

"Well, Mother; you know I 'neglect my family,' and I've been looking into it. I don't see but the house is in pretty good order, and we have all excellent appetites, and the children are pretty well clothed. There seems to be nothing actually lacking for the comfort of this family, unless it is a tidy. We are really deficient in that luxury, or necessity. Perhaps I ought to set to work."

Grandma saw the point, and laughed till her capstrings shook like leaves. But Mr. Leymon took a more serious view of the matter.

"I beg of you, don't!" he said earnestly. "Whatever you may be tempted to do in revenge in this world, *don't* make a tidy. If I had the naming of them, I'd call them 'untidies'! If they are not the torment of a man, I don't know what is! I never go to Mr. Colman's but when I get out of a chair there is one sticking to my back and one to each elbow, and I always have an uncomfortable feeling that there *may* be one hanging to my hair."

And the criticisms that troubled Mrs. Leymon so little were infinitely more than balanced by the blessed rewards of the work. She always remembered a certain summer afternoon, when the firstfruits of a *glorious* harvest—the extent of which can only be known in eternity—were gathered in. It was one of those homes that had been low, destitute, unclean, and awful! It was a mother, and she lay dying; and on the table but a few feet from her stood a little coffin— neat, tasteful, delicate—and the baby, with golden head, sleeping peacefully within, was as sweet and as pure and as white-robed as any mother's darling that was ever laid away in coffined bed. In her baby hand she clasped a small, white, fragrant bud; and the mother's eyes, over which the film of death was creeping, sought ever and anon that tiny coffin, and as often as she saw it she smiled. And among her last words on earth were these:

"Baby and I are safe. Baby is gone where *he* said 'Suffer them to come,' and I am going. He is waiting for me. And there is a clean white dress there for me—for *me!* And I"—the voice fails, stops, gathers strength for one last effort—"and I should never have known anything about it at all, or about *him,* if it hadn't been for you!"

And there was brought another coffin, neat and decorous, large enough to receive mother and child. And there were pure flowers strewn up and down the quiet forms lying therein, and around the coffin a hymn was sung:

> *"Asleep in Jesus, blessed sleep!*
> *From which none ever wake to weep.*
> *A calm and undisturbed repose,*
> *Unbroken by the last of foes."*

And the minister read from the Bible, and among his selections came these words: "Precious in the sight of the Lord is the death of his saints." What! over that coffin? holding that sad, sinful, almost lost mother! Holding that baby! child of the lowliest and lowest of earth! Yes, indeed! "Precious in the sight of the Lord is the death of his saints." "Ye that are weary and heavy laden." "Beloved of God." "Called to be saints." "Come unto me!" And they had gone.

And Mrs. Leymon had risen away above criticism, pettiness, envy, and misunderstanding, into the realm of Christlike work and Christ-given joy.

THE END

## *Don't miss these Grace Livingston Hill Library romance novels by Isabella Alden*